THE
PURR-FECT
SCOOP

THE
PURR-FECT
SCOOP

Coco Simon

Simon Spotlight
New York London Toronto Sydney New Delhi

This book is a work of fiction. Any references to historical events, real people, or real places are used fictitiously. Other names, characters, places, and events are products of the author's imagination, and any resemblance to actual events or places or persons, living or dead, is entirely coincidental.

SIMON SPOTLIGHT
An imprint of Simon & Schuster Children's Publishing Division
1230 Avenue of the Americas, New York, New York 10020
This Simon Spotlight edition August 2018
Copyright © 2018 by Simon & Schuster, Inc.
All rights reserved, including the right of reproduction in whole or in part in any form.
SIMON SPOTLIGHT and colophon are registered trademarks of Simon & Schuster, Inc.
For information about special discounts for bulk purchases, please contact Simon & Schuster Special Sales at 1-866-506-1949 or business@simonandschuster.com.
Text by Elizabeth Doyle Carey
Series designed by Hannah Frece
Cover designed by Alisa Coburn and Hannah Frece
Cover illustrations by Alisa Coburn
The text of this book was set in Bembo Std.
Manufactured in the United States of America 0718 OFF
10 9 8 7 6 5 4 3 2 1
ISBN 978-1-5344-2893-5 (hc)
ISBN 978-1-5344-2892-8 (pbk)
ISBN 978-1-5344-2894-2 (eBook)
Library of Congress Catalog Card Number 2018948378

CHAPTER ONE

A SECRET BETWEEN SISTERS

I knew it had to be there somewhere! I just had to find it. I tied my long, brown hair into a ponytail to get it out of my way, and then I began searching slowly but surely, room by room, throughout the house.

My first stop was our clean but messy bright yellow kitchen, where I circled the cluttered table, sifted carefully through the pile of newspapers and magazines for recycling, and roamed around the packed countertops and the jumbly kitchen island and even into the little closet with the washer and dryer, but no luck. I was desperate. I'd borrowed a comic book from my friend Cecelia, and I had to give it back to her at our comic book club meeting after school on Monday. That gave me only two days to find it. I had no clue where it could be.

My *abuela* said that the key to finding things was that you had to *really* look, even in places where you thought you'd already checked or places where you couldn't even imagine the thing being.

I went all through the living/dining room area, lifting sofa cushions, flipping through all the colorful needlepoint throw pillows my dad had made, peeking behind the bright watercolors of birds my mom did for fun, looking underneath the box lid of the half-done jigsaw puzzle on the dining room table. Nothing! I wandered into my parents' home office, but it was so immaculate that I could see at a glance that the comic book wasn't on either of their back-to-back desktops or the low chest that held copies of their research and patients' files. The only place where my parents were neat was in their offices, both at home and at work. I couldn't really criticize them for messiness, though; I was messy and disorganized too. We all always thought we'd get back to a project, or find some time to clean up later, or organize our things, and then we would get busy and forget about it and never clean up.

Upstairs I went into my parents' bedroom, where

their bed was still unmade and clothing was strewn across chairbacks and the small love seat by the window. A large oil painting of Cuban storefronts, by my dad's dad, hung proudly above my mom's dresser. She loved that picture, but my dad didn't. Both of their families had come to America when they were babies, and while my mom was dying to go back for a visit, my dad said he never would. He didn't even like to talk about Cuba.

I sighed. No sign of the comic book in their room, or in their bathroom—thank goodness, because all their towels were damp and heaped in a pile. If the comic had been there, it would surely have been ruined. I knew it wasn't in my room because that was what had started this whole search. That left only one more possibility: my twin sister's room.

Unfortunately, Isabel's room was currently off-limits to me.

Isa's door was closed tightly, something she'd taken to doing since school had started this year. I wouldn't have been surprised if the door was locked. She'd left earlier that afternoon, but I wasn't sure when she was going to return, and I dared not enter without her permission or I'd face her wrath.

I stood on the landing outside her door, my arms folded, my foot tapping in place as I thought. Finally I decided.

I put my hand on her doorknob.

Did I dare open the door?

Slowly, slowly, I turned the handle, my hand shaking a little. The door was not locked, it turned out, and the handle turned easily.

My eyes strained for a glimpse of a room I hadn't seen inside in more than six weeks. And then . . . *BANG!* The back door slammed downstairs!

I pulled Isabel's door closed, released the handle, and scurried back to my room, where I flung myself onto my bed, trying to look natural.

"Hello?" I called. I assumed it was Isa because my parents had returned to their clinic after our big Saturday lunch, as usual.

There was no reply, only the sound of firm footsteps stomping across the floor below and then heading up the stairs.

"Isa?" I called.

Suddenly she was at my door. "Were you just in my room?" she demanded.

"What? Me? No! Seriously? Jeez!" *How on earth had she known?*

Isabel was carrying a big brown box. It had holes cut all around it, and something inside was making noise.

"What's in the box?" I asked.

She hesitated and then turned on her heel and went to her room without answering me.

I waited a second, and then, intrigued, I stood to follow her. She opened her door, flipped on the lights with her elbow, and crossed the room to her desk. I was right behind her, and it surprised me that she didn't slam the door in my face like she usually would have. I stayed in the doorway anyway, just to be safe.

Isabel and I were technically identical twins, but no one mixed us up anymore. When we were little, our mom would dress us in similar (never identical) outfits. I always had everything in pink and Isa in purple, even our bedrooms. If I got a doll with a red dress, Isa would get the exact same one but in a blue dress. All through the previous year we had been really identical. But over the last few months, especially since school had started, we'd grown to be very different. We weren't as close as we used to be. Things were really different now.

Isabel had changed her style—from preppy cute to wearing all-black clothes and changing her hairstyle constantly: dyeing it blue, putting it in cornrows, and then wearing her most recent rocker chick mullet. Meanwhile, my hair was still long and brown and wavy, and I wore bright and flowing clothes, kind of hippyish. You'd have to look pretty carefully to see that we were twins.

Isabel placed the box carefully on her desk, turned on her gooseneck lamp, and peeked inside the box's flaps.

"What is it?" I said, getting more curious by the minute.

Isabel turned and looked at me, considering me for a minute. Then with a little smile on her face, she said, "Come see."

I crossed the room, swiveling my head from side to side to look at all the redecorating she'd done in the previous few weeks. Unlike my room and most of the rest of the house, Isa's room was as neat as a pin. But she'd covered her purple walls completely with rock band posters and photos cut out of magazines—race cars, futuristic skyscrapers, weird

6

artwork. My eyes were spinning like pinwheels, trying to quickly take it all in during the quick journey to her desk.

I peered over her shoulder, not knowing what to expect. When I spied the box's contents, I gasped and reared back.

"Whoa!" I said. "That's a snake!"

Isabel smiled more widely and reached her hands into the box.

"Careful! It might bite you!" I said, clutching my hand to my chest. Despite being the child of two veterinarians, I was not a snake person.

But apparently Isabel now was.

"It's a corn snake. Corn snakes don't bite," she said confidently.

She pulled her hands out of the box, and in them sat an orange striped snake, coiled neatly into a pile of snakiness.

"OMG. What is that disgusting thing doing here?" I said, jumping backward about four feet.

Isabel's smile faded into its new usual scowl, and she turned her back on me, cradling the snake. "It lives here now," she said quietly but with a hint of pride in her voice. "With me. I adopted it."

I realized I'd just made a major blunder when I'd called the snake disgusting. I knew I had to apologize or this would escalate into a huge fight, like all our disagreements lately, and I needed Isa's help to find the comic book. She was the only good finder in the family, and the odds were high that the book was in her room, anyway. While her back was turned to me, I scanned every surface, but I didn't see it; not that that meant anything. If Isa had the comic, it would be neatly alphabetized and filed away on her bookcase.

I sighed. "I'm sorry, Isa. It just scared me. I'm . . . I'm just not really a snake person."

"Well, I am. Just because we're identical doesn't mean we're *identical*!"

I put my hands up in surrender. "Jeez, sorry. I never thought we were."

"Look, just don't tell Mom and Dad, okay? I really want it, and, well, you know how they are about pets. . . ."

Our parents had laid down the law about pets a long time before. They were willing to foster animals briefly, and we had done so many times over the years. (Our most recent foster had been a tiny, adorable shih tzu called Gizmo whom my friend Amber had wound up adopting.) But despite the many, many times that Isa and I had begged to keep the fostered animals, our parents had always maintained that we did not need any permanent pets at home. They said that it was too much work for them to take care of animals all day at their clinic and then come home and do it again at night. In a moment of weakness my mom had once admitted that she'd made the rule early on because our dad was such a softie that our house would have looked like Noah's ark if she'd let him start keeping animals.

"Do you really think you can have a secret pet? That seems like a bad idea," I said.

Isabel's eyes were huge and earnest. "Please, Sisi? Please let it be our secret?"

Sisi! Isabel hadn't called me "Sisi" in ages. I melted. "I guess. I think it's a bad idea, but I won't say anything. At least not for now."

Isabel released a long breath she must have been holding for a while. "Thank you."

Just then the doorbell rang downstairs. Isabel looked at me, alarmed, but then her face changed as she seemed to realize who it was.

"Could you go get the door for me? It's Francie— the girl I'm adopting the snake from. She has the tank and all the gear and stuff. I need to stay up here with the snake, just in case Mom and Dad randomly come home. I don't want them to see Naga."

I raised my eyebrows, which were thick and dark and made quite a statement when I used them like that.

"Please, Sierra? Answer the door?" Isabel begged, her own dark eyebrows knit together on her forehead.

This was practically the longest conversation we'd had in weeks, and I liked having Isabel need my help. Plus, if she felt like she owed me one, she'd probably help me look for my comic book.

"Okay," I said, and I dashed downstairs.

I opened the door to find a redheaded girl I recognized from the grade above me at school.

"Hi," I said.

The girl looked at me in confusion. I don't think I look that much like Isabel anymore, but I guess I do. When people see me for the first time, they still sometimes do a double take. I smiled. "I'm Sierra, Isabel's twin. She sent me down because she's busy with the . . . ah . . . *snake* . . . upstairs." I whispered the word "snake" as if my parents had listening devices everywhere.

"Oh! Hi. I'm Francie. Okay, so this is the gear for Naga." In her arms were a big fish tank with a lamp and some other electrical equipment, plus a little bowl, a small cavelike shelter, and more.

"Ooh!" I said, spying a white Chinese take-out container in the tank. "Does Naga eat Chinese food?"

Francie looked perplexed, and then she laughed. "No! Those are frozen baby mice. *That's* what she likes to eat! Mice cream! Mice-icles!"

Oh no. I actually almost gagged. "O-kaaaay."

Francie looked at me seriously. "Corn snakes are constrictors—they like to wrap around their prey and strangle it, then eat it. Pretty soon Naga will have to be fed small live animals. . . ."

I felt weak. I think my jaw must've dropped open, because Francie was suddenly eager to leave.

She thrust the gear into my arms. "Thanks so much for taking her. My parents just did not want a snake in the house, but they were really happy to hear she was coming to live with two vets."

"Right," I said. *But the vets don't know it yet,* I added silently. "Well, thanks. Come back and visit anytime!"

Francie turned and walked down the path, waving as she went. She couldn't get away fast enough. I think she was relieved to be done with the snake. Or maybe she was just glad to be rid of the frozen baby mice. She practically skipped down the sidewalk.

"Hmmm," I said, closing the front door with my foot. "I bet we won't see her again." I held the tank away from me at arm's length. If I caught even one whiff of the "mice-icles," I would surely be sick.

Upstairs Isabel startled when I came in.

"It's just me. Relax," I said. I put the gear down on her bed. "Um, do you know what this critter eats?"

Isabel smiled. "Yup."

I shuddered. "Are you going to keep them in the freezer, like, with all of our food?"

She nodded. "Uh-huh."

I sighed. "It's a good thing our parents are so messy. They'll never notice."

"I know. But they might notice the tank. I'm going to work to get this all set up before they come home. It's going in my closet."

In the closet. Well, at least that was good. That meant there would be at least two doors between me and the snake.

"Well, at least Mom and Dad are extra busy right now. That should buy you some time this afternoon,"

I said. Our parents were in the middle of renovating one of their examining rooms and their lab area. Though they usually worked seven days a week, things right then were crazier than ever, with the renovations going on after clinic hours, making their days really long.

"Mm-hmm," agreed Isabel.

She put Naga back into the cardboard box, carefully closed it, and weighed down the top with a heavy book. Then she came over to the bed to assess what Francie had brought. I hovered in the doorway, unsure if I should stay or go. Isabel never hung out with me or my friends anymore, and her new friends were all kinds of weird: either punk and a little scary-looking or soccer-maniac boys from her all-boy travel team. She and I used to have so many little secrets and rituals. We were Team P, the Perez sisters. *Sisters for life,* we would always say. Then we'd do a fist bump and pulse our hands away like jellyfish. But that had all dried up lately. Team P was on a permanent vacation.

I was enjoying feeling close again for the moment, so I tried to stretch it out. "Remember when we really wanted to keep that German shepherd puppy?" I said.

Isabel smiled wistfully. "Roman. He was so handsome."

"Yeah," I agreed, remembering how much we'd loved snuggling with him on the sofa in front of the TV. "But he did have that peeing problem. . . ."

Isabel laughed—a quick, short laugh, but still a laugh. "And when he peed on Mom and Dad's bed, they finally said they'd found him a new family! Funny timing, right?"

"I wish we had a pet," I said with a sigh.

"Well, now we do!" cheered Isabel.

"Humph. A snake's not really a pet. I've always wanted something furry to snuggle with."

"I think a snake's a pet. I'll snuggle with Naga," said Isabel defiantly.

"Right. Sorry," I agreed, thinking, *Whatever!* Things were starting to get a little dicey, so I figured I'd better strike while I still could. "Any chance you'd help me look for a comic book I lost? It's called *Ms. Marvelous*."

Without even looking up, Isabel jerked her thumb at her bookcase. "Bottom shelf. Under the letter *M* for 'Marvelous.' Sorry. I saw it in the living room and thought Mom had gotten it for me."

Bingo! I went to her shelf and pulled it right out. While I was there, I noticed lots of books I'd never seen before.

"Hey! When did you get all into graphic novels?" I asked, fanning them out and showing them to Isabel.

Isabel shrugged. "I don't know. My friends are into them."

"Yuck!" I said, turning the pages.

Isabel got annoyed then. "You know what? Just . . . Can you just leave? I don't need you in here being all goody-two-shoes and judging my stuff. Okay? We're not the same person anymore. So just skedaddle! Get out!" Isabel grabbed all the books from my hands. "Shoo!"

I raised my hands in the air in surrender. "Sor-*ry*!" I said, grabbing my friend's comic book and leaving the room. "And I'm not a Goody Two-shoes!"

"Ha!" was the reply before the door slammed shut behind me.

I found myself standing alone again in the upstairs hall, but at least this time I had the comic book in my hand. Mission accomplished.

CHAPTER TWO
KITTENS!

After the snake drama with Isa, I was so excited to be out of the house that night and hanging with my forever best friends, Allie Shear and Tamiko Sato, that I was practically giddy. They weren't my sisters, I guess, but they felt like they could be. And lately they had felt more like my sisters than my real sister had.

Tamiko was super into style and customizing things. She was really creative and energetic, and she was obsessed with baseball, especially Japanese baseball.

Allie was bookish and sweet and a really good student. Her parents had just split up, so she had had to move houses and change schools.

I was the "spacey" one. Mom always told me that

I wasn't and that I shouldn't label myself, but I kind of *was* spacey. I could never remember anything, and time always got away from me. I wasn't a star student, but I did okay in school. My label, even though I wasn't supposed to use labels, was a "joiner." I joined everything, and because I was so involved in things, I had a ton of friends. And because I was "spacey" to start out with, sometimes it was hard for me to manage all my commitments, because I'd forget when I had promised to meet people or due dates for projects. That was where my friends usually stepped in to help me. It used to be that Isa would step in and cover for me, but not anymore.

Since Allie had moved to another town and another school, the three of us made an effort to get together every week. Plus, every Sunday afternoon we all worked together at Allie's mom's new ice cream parlor, Molly's. We called ourselves the Sprinkle Sunday sisters.

That night Tamiko's parents took us to this really cool spot in a strip mall a couple of towns over. It was a Sushirrito restaurant, where they sold sushi burritos (and Mexican-inspired sushi). Tamiko's parents sat at a separate table at the other end of the restaurant so that we could have some private time, just the three of us Sprinkle Sunday sisters.

While we waited for our number to be called with our orders, we caught up on the week.

Tamiko was showing us these pointy lollipops she'd found to use in the unicorn sundaes at the ice cream shop. The lollipops had multicolored swirls that twirled around the top of a stick, which would represent the horn of the unicorn. She'd found a place to get them wholesale, and with the help of her brother, Kai, she had created a PowerPoint presentation for Mrs. Shear on the pros of buying these candies. "I'm all about style, innovation, *and* the bottom line," was her pitch. Based on her thrifted punk outfit—a blue ballet tutu over some fleecy red leggings, and an old fake-leopard-print jacket—I'd say she was true to her word.

"Cool," I said, "but can we not talk shop anymore? I want to really hear what's going on with everyone."

Allie smiled, because what I really meant was that I wanted to know what was going on with her. It was weird to go from seeing someone every day to only seeing them once a week, and I was really curious about what was going on in Allie's life.

"Well, I have some news," Allie said. "Get it, news? I have the perfect name for my column in the school paper!"

"That's so cool!" Tamiko said. "What's it called?"

"Get the Scoop!" Allie said triumphantly. "Get it?"

"We got it!" Tamiko and I said at the same time, laughing.

"Every week I do an interview with someone in the community," she said. "Then I ask them about their favorite ice cream flavors for Get the Scoop. And of course I give Molly's a plug."

"Fifty-nine?" intoned the voice over the loud-speaker.

"Oooh! That's us!" cried Tamiko, jumping up like she'd just won the lottery. "I'll get it."

Tamiko was back in seconds with a tray piled high with burritos. She doled them out, and we began to unwrap the rolls.

I'd ordered a California Crunch burrito. The tortilla was filled with shrimp tempura, guacamole, rice, spicy mayo, cucumbers, and crunchy fried onions. My mouth watered as I saw the two neatly sliced halves in the wrapper. I was starting to lift one half to my mouth for a bite when Tamiko's hand shot out and stopped me before I could taste it.

"No! We need to post it!"

My mouth was open and watering for that first delectable bite. "What?"

"Hello? Social media? Put it down. I need to take photos," she said.

Sighing, I placed the roll back onto its wrapper on the table. Allie and I exchanged an amused look as she did the same.

Tamiko busied herself styling the food and positioning it *just so* for her phone camera. She'd gotten a yellowtail roll, and Allie's was the Chicken Firecracker. Tamiko was standing on her seat, trying to get a good overhead shot, when her mother walked by to pick up her order. "Tamiko! What on earth? Get down! Where are your manners?" she said, shaking her head.

Tamiko grinned, stepped down, and turned to follow her mom to the counter to check out what her parents had gotten. Allie and I didn't waste a minute. We reached out, grabbed our rolls, and took enormous bites out of them. Then, smiling through our full mouths, we placed our rolls back onto the wrappers.

Tamiko came right back, smiling, but her smile faded as she looked at the now-messy rolls and then at each of us. She sighed in disgust and said, "Okay, you win. Just eat them!"

Allie and I laughed and dove for our food again, which we chowed happily. We continued chatting between bites.

"All right. I was saving my big news," I said. "Are you ready?"

They looked at me in alarm. Ever since Allie had announced her parents' divorce a couple of months before, we'd all been a little skittish. "Oh, relax! It's not that big—actually, it's small news. Isabel brought home a pet snake today."

"Eeew!" said Allie.

"Cool!" said Tamiko, both reactions that I could have predicted.

"I agree with Allie," I said.

"What kind?" asked Tamiko, flicking her straight black bangs out of her eyes.

"A corn snake. Have you ever heard of it?" I asked.

Tamiko nodded confidently and picked up her phone to scroll. "Corn snakes are really in right now. They're all over the place. It's because they come in

21

such cool colors and markings. Was it orange?"

"Yes!" I said in surprise, though I should have known that Tamiko would know all about anything trendy like this.

She held up a photo. "Like this?"

I nodded and shivered, thinking of it living in my house. "Yup."

"They're really beautiful," said Tamiko. "So after all these years your parents finally let you get a pet, and it's a *snake*?"

I cleared my throat uncomfortably. "Well. Actually. Um . . ."

There was a pause.

Allie looked at me carefully. "They don't know, do they?"

I shook my head. "Nope."

"But Isabel's going to tell them, right?" pressed Allie.

I grimaced. "I guess not. She thinks they'll make her get rid of it, so she wants to keep it a secret."

Tamiko winced. "Yikes. That'll be hard. The one thing about pet snakes is that they always escape. Then everyone will have to know."

"Oh no! I hope not!" I said with another shudder.

"Wait," said Allie. "How can she *not* tell them? I mean, it's another living thing in the house. Plus, your parents are vets. They'd want to know about an animal living with them."

I shrugged. "I don't know what she'll do."

"But she should tell them. Or *you* should."

"No way, Sunday Sister! I'm not telling them!" I said, folding my arms across my chest. "Isabel would kill me! She'd put the snake in my bed!" I laughed.

Allie folded her arms now. "They should know. You can't hide a living creature in a house without permission, especially when it breaks your parents' main rule about no pets. It's wrong."

I sighed. "I know, Allie. But what can I do?"

"Nothing!" said Tamiko. "Just stay out of it. It will all work out! You don't want to get in trouble too."

But Allie was shaking her head. "Whatever you do, just don't lie to your parents. Lies make everything worse."

Famous last words, I thought later as my parents sat Isabel and me down in the living room for a family meeting before bed.

Phew, I thought. *Isabel told them immediately, and*

23

now we're going to have the "no pets" talk again and find a new home for Naga. But I was wrong.

"Girls, we need your help," my mom began. "A client brought in an abandoned mama cat today with three tiny kittens."

"Awwww," I said. "How old?"

"We think they're around five or six weeks old," said my dad. "They're about the size of my hand." He held one hand up.

My mom continued. "We're going to foster them, but we don't think it's a good idea for them to stay at the clinic since we aren't housing any animals during the construction. The renovation is making too much of a mess. If we brought them home after they have their checkups on Monday—assuming they pass and are healthy—would you be willing to look after them while you're here and we're at work?"

"Totally!" I cried, jumping on my mom to hug her. "That would be so fun! Oh, can we keep one kitten? Please?"

My mom shook her head. "Sorry, but you know the rule. . . ."

"No pets," we all intoned, except maybe Isa. I didn't dare look at her to see if she was saying it too, but she did look uncomfortable when I glanced at her a moment later.

I thought this was the perfect time for her to make the announcement about Naga, so when my mom went to get her phone to show us pictures of the kittens and my dad went to grab himself a cold drink, I stared daggers at Isa until she raised her eyes and looked at me. I wiggled my eyebrows and tipped my head toward the kitchen, where our parents were, as if to say, *Tell them about the snake now,* but Isa just defiantly looked away.

I sighed heavily, making a big coughing noise with the back of my throat, trying to get her to look at me again, but she wouldn't. *All right, sister,* I said inside my head, hoping she'd hear me through some twin telepathy. *You're on your own.*

My mom returned with her phone and her reading glasses, and my dad with his water, and they called me and Isa over to the sofa to snuggle in and scroll through the pics.

I oohed and aahed over every photo, but Isabel was pretty quiet.

"What do you think, Izzy-boo?" My dad called Isabel by his baby nickname for her. "Cute?"

Isabel sighed. "I'm just not that into cute and fuzzy stuff anymore, Dad."

My dad made funny wide eyes at her. "What? Since when? Just a few weeks ago you were begging us to keep that shih tzu! Anyway, who's not into cute and fuzzy? Next thing, you'll be telling me you hate rainbows, and cupcakes, and pony rides!"

Isabel was trying hard not to smile, and she stayed serious long enough to say, "I *do* hate those things." But my dad dove over and tickled her until she screamed with laughter, yelling, "Mercy! Mercy!"

He wouldn't stop until he got her to yell, "I love kittens!"

She was gasping and laughing along with the rest of us when he finally let her go. I hadn't seen her laugh like that since the previous spring, I think.

"I thought so!" he said, mock-indignantly.

She jumped to a chair far away and said, "But I really hate them!"

My dad fake-lunged at her, and she shrieked with laughter, then said, "Okay, okay. I love them! No I don't!" They joked back and forth for a few minutes, and we all were laughing.

It was the most fun we'd had as a family in a

while, and the kittens weren't even at our house yet. Going upstairs for bed, I wanted to tell Isa that this would be the perfect time to tell our parents about Naga—while everyone was in a good mood and feeling close, and before the secret had gone on too long. But when she said "Good night, Sisi" upstairs, using my childhood nickname again, I couldn't quite bring myself to say anything about her secret.

CHAPTER THREE

LATE AGAIN—NO EXCUSES

After lunch on Sunday—as I was simultaneously working on my science project, despairing about all the extracurricular stuff I had to do the following week, sending e-mails about the school food drive, and sorting my laundry—Isa appeared in my doorway.

"Sierra, can you help me for a minute?" She spoke quietly, even though our parents had gone to work right after church that morning.

"Is this about our little friend?" I asked, peering over the top of my notebook at her.

"Ha-ha, very funny, but yes. I need to put some newspaper in the bottom of her tank. I forgot to get it from downstairs yesterday, and then I couldn't grab it once Mom and Dad were home."

I sighed. "I don't like being part of your sneaki-ness," I said, dropping the notebook to my side. "But I'll help you again." It felt good to be needed by Isa (and, let's face it, also to have her owe me one). Plus, I'd rather do anything other than my homework.

I swung my legs off the bed and knocked over a pile of laundry as I did. "Ugh."

"Come on, hurry! You never know when they'll be back on Sundays!" she pleaded.

I waded through a pile of my gear for mountain-eering club, and two shopping bags full of cans that I'd collected for the food drive, and out my door to the hall.

Once we were in her room, Isabel shut the door behind us and went quickly to her closet. She'd rearranged her furniture to hide the extension cord leading into her closed closet. It was pretty clever the way she'd done it, actually. No one would notice. And since our parents had declared us old enough to clean our own rooms the previous summer, there was little chance my mom would be doing anything in Isabel's closet, or maybe even her room, for a long time.

Isabel opened the door, and a golden light spilled out. It was almost magical.

"Wow!" I said, drawn to the tank where a heat lamp radiated warm light.

I knelt to look inside. The water bowl and lamp and some other equipment were all neatly set up, and Naga was curled inside her little hiding cave.

"Hi, Naga!" I said, trying to promote interspecies friendship as well as family harmony.

"Okay, I'm going to take her out now," said Isa. "Do you want to do the newspaper, or do you want to hold her?"

"Uh . . . duh! Newspaper!" I said. "Nothing personal, but I am not into slimy critters."

Isabel sighed and said, "Fine, but she's nice to hold. She's not slimy at all. She's dry and cool, and her skin is very smooth."

I snorted. "I'll take your word for it."

Isabel knelt down and removed some heavy books that were on top of the tank lid. Then she removed the lid and reached in. I couldn't even watch, I was so sure that Isabel was going to get bitten. I looked away and asked, "Is Naga a big reader?"

"Huh?" said Isabel.

"The books?" I prompted.

"Oh. Those are to keep her from escaping. Snakes

are really good at pushing out through the tiniest cracks. You have to always assume they could get out. I read that on the internet."

I shuddered. "Great. Just what I want in a neighbor. So, what do you want me to do with the paper?"

"Okay. Just rip it into long strips, please. Uh-huh, yup. Just like that."

I tore the sheets into long strips and placed them in a growing pile. "How many pages?"

"Mmm. I think, like, five?"

"Five!"

"Well, I don't know. Let's see."

I tore in silence for a minute. Once I had a decent pile of three ripped sheets' worth of strips, I asked, "Should we start with this?"

"Fine."

I reached into the tank to lift out the little cave, and then I saw it. The dead mouse was sitting there in the tank, under where the cave had been, its little feet curled up in front of its chest and its little buckteeth sticking out of its snout. I shrieked, dropped the cave, jumped up, and ran to the door, in full body shudders.

"Ugh, ugh, ugh, ugh!" I cried.

Isa smirked. "It's just a little mouse. And it's dead!"

31

I shivered. "Yuck. That is so nasty! Snakes are so gross!"

"Kittens could eat baby mice too, you know!"

"Yes, but not on a regular basis. And they eat them in the wild, if at all, so you never have to see it happen."

Isabel sighed. "Do you want to hold Naga over there, and I'll finish the tank myself?"

"Gosh. I just don't know which is worse, the dead mouse or the slippery snake!"

"Thanks a lot," said Isabel, and by the wounded look on her face, I knew I'd gone too far.

"I'm sorry, Isa. I didn't mean it. I know you like her a lot. . . ." I took a huge breath, and then I said, "I'll hold the . . . Naga. Just tell me what to do."

Isabel brightened. "Really? Okay. Thanks. Look, just put both hands out together, kind of cupped, like this." I followed her directions. "Right. Now I'm going to put her into your hands. Please don't drop her. She could get really hurt if you drop her. Okay? She's just a baby."

"Oh no, oh no, oh no," I said as she placed Naga into my hands. Naga's body was cool and dense, kind of heavy for her size, and Isa was right: she wasn't

32

slimy at all. Her skin was smooth like a stone, almost, and the muscles under her skin were strong and firm. Her head moved around as her tongue darted in and out of her mouth. She explored my wrists and sleeve and then settled into a perfect coil in the palms of my hands. "I cannot believe I'm holding a snake right now!" I said in shock.

Isabel was working quickly, but she glanced back at me. "Good job. Stay strong. You can do it."

"Why do they do that licking thing with their tongue going in and out?" I asked.

"It's how they smell," replied Isa.

"And she's not going to bite me, right?"

"I promise," said Isa, deftly distributing the newspaper strips across the bottom of the tank.

"How do you know so much about snakes?" I asked.

Isabel shrugged. "From reading about them. And my friends at school."

"Do they have pet snakes?" I asked. I didn't really know any of her school friends. They were all pretty new friends, since she'd stopped hanging with me and my friends a year or so before.

"Some do, like Thomas and Reed."

I'd never heard of either of those people, but I didn't want to ask right then. I was enjoying the closeness of the moment with Isa and didn't want to wreck it. It felt like Team P was on the verge of rekindling, and I didn't want to jinx the reunion.

I looked down at Naga, now asleep in my hands. Her skin was incredible up close—an alternating pattern of dark red, black, and light orange bands that gave an overall impression of the color orange but up close was intricate and beautiful.

"She's really beautiful, Isa," I said softly.

Isabel looked up at me and smiled. "I think so too."

I took a deep breath. "If you want to play this right, though, you're going to have to tell Mom and Dad. Because if they find out on their own, they'll be too mad to let you keep her. Why would you risk that?"

Isabel repositioned the cave and, I imagine, the mouse–icle, back in the tank and then reached out her hands for Naga. I handed her over, surprised by how I missed the weight of her once I'd let her go.

"I just don't want them to say no," she said quietly. "I have to choose my time very carefully—"

Time! Oh no!

I raced to my room to look at my phone. 12:50! And Mrs. Shear wanted us to be at Molly's by 12:45 for a one o'clock shift! I was already five minutes late!

Hurriedly I pulled on my socks and threw a tunic over my leggings and tank top. Hopping in place as I rushed my sneakers on, I called to Isabel, "I'm late. I've got to go to work! Shoot! I am going to be in so much trouble for being late again!"

Isabel called, "I'm sorry! Thank you for helping me!" and it warmed my heart so much that it almost made my tardiness worth it.

"You're welcome!" I called back, feeling a glow of sisterly love that I hadn't felt in literally months.

It was funny how that little snake—the unlikeliest of creatures—had drawn us close again.

"I know, I know! I'm so sorry!" I said as I raced into Molly's at 1:19. I ducked into the rear of the store ("backstage," we called it) and washed up. Then I raced out, tying on my apron as I went.

Out front there was a huge line all the way to the front door, mostly of very tall people in uniforms.

"Is this an entire basketball team?" I joked to Allie,

but her blue eyes were stormy. She was straight-lipped and didn't reply.

"Next!" was all she said.

Uh-oh.

Tamiko breezed by me to deliver an elaborate unicorn sundae to a customer. "Seriously, dude?" she whispered to me. "After all the talks about lateness?" Her high black ponytail swished from side to side as she rushed by me.

I sighed. What could I say in my own defense? *Oh, hey, my sister is finally being nice to me again after months of iciness, and I'm so desperate to be her friend again that I lost track of time?*

Humph.

I probably could have said that, actually. After all, Tamiko and Allie were my besties, and they knew every living detail of my life. But they had been depending on me, and I had let them down by being late.

"Next?" I called, and I was off and running.

Once the post-lunch rush had finally petered out, Allie said, "Sierra? Can we talk?" She jerked her thumb backstage, and I followed her there.

"You're in *trouble*," whispered Tamiko in a sing-songy voice as I passed her. I gave her a good snap with the dishtowel I was holding and kept on walking.

"Mommy! Sierra hit me!" Tamiko fake-cried.

In the back, Allie's face was bright red. "You know what? The thing I hate the most about your being late is that I have to tell my mom about it. It's so awful! I hate doing it, and that makes me even *madder*!" She ran her hands through her wavy dark brown hair in frustration.

"I'm so sorry. I really am. I just—"

Allie put her hands up. "Sierra. I know there was a reason. I'm sure it was probably a pretty good one. It always is—"

"I was helping—"

But she cut me off again and continued. "I know. You're very helpful. It's just . . . every time you're helping someone *else*, you're letting me and Tamiko down! When do *we* come first? When does *work* come first?"

She had a point. There wasn't anything I could say.

"I'm sorry," I said.

Allie sighed. "I know you are. I just wish it wouldn't keep happening. We're a team. The Sprinkle

Sunday sisters, remember? When you're late, you're letting down the team and we don't work as well. We're a well-oiled machine, and when part of the machine isn't here, well . . ."

I squared my shoulders and took a deep breath. "I won't be late again. I promise. I will make you and Tamiko and work my priority on Sundays. In fact, I'll come in early—"

"Actually, that's what I was going to say. You realize that every time you're late, you're kind of stealing from the store, right?"

That stopped me in my tracks. "What?"

Allie nodded. "Yes. Because my mom pays you for the full four hours, but if you only work three and a half, you're taking money you didn't earn. Get it? It's wrong. It's . . . stealing. So I'm going to ask you to please come in a half hour early next week to work it off. Or . . . or . . ." Allie sighed. "I really don't want to do it, but I'll have to tell my mom. Okay?"

I nodded, not liking to think of myself as a *thief*, of all things! And Allie was going to rat me out! Where was the loyalty?

"Got it. Sorry," I said, swallowing hard.

Allie sighed again. "Okay, thanks. I feel so much better now that I've gotten all this off my chest. I just don't like feeling cheated. And also, I don't like feeling overwhelmed. We were shorthanded today when we had a rush, and people might leave and not come back if the wait is too long. The shop is too new for us to expect people to stand in long lines and wait for our ice cream. You know?"

"Yeah."

Just then Tamiko popped her head into the back. "Everything okay back here?"

Allie and I looked at each other, then at Tamiko. I shrugged, and Allie said, "Yes. We're all good. Right, Sierra?"

I said, "I guess."

"Awww, come on. Hug it out, bros!" teased Tamiko. At first Allie and I just looked at each other awkwardly, but Tamiko kept saying it until we hugged. I knew Allie was still my friend, but I didn't feel like things were one hundred percent back to normal yet. There was still a little bit of tension between us.

"Now come back up front and tell us all about the kitties that you texted us about!" Tamiko said.

Back in the ice cream parlor area, Allie put some good music on to energize us, and we did the post-rush cleanup. We divvied up the tasks: refilling the topping bins, mopping the floor, cleaning the counter- and tabletops, rinsing out the milkshake machines, swapping out the empty ice cream buckets, even cleaning the bathroom. (I took that one on as a kind of payback for my lateness.) We had the place superclean in no time. I worked extra hard and extra fast to make up for my lateness, and Allie was appreciative.

While we worked, I filled them in on the kittens.

"Hey! Just like a kitten café!" said Tamiko.

"What's that?" asked Allie, leaning on her broom.

Tamiko pulled out her phone and began thumbing through screens. "In Japan there's this trend of pet cafés—different themes, like bunnies, kittens, cats, whatever—and you go get coffee and pay the entrance fee, and you can sit and play with the animals for as long as you like."

"Cool," I said.

Tamiko nodded. "The bunny one is really popular in Tokyo. It has five floors. And there's even a pug café!" Tamiko was obsessed with pugs.

"That sounds awesome," said Allie. "Is there a snake café?" She grinned at me wickedly. I sighed.

"She *still* didn't tell your parents?" asked Allie disapprovingly.

I shrugged and winced at the same time. "What can I say?"

"Tell her to do it!" insisted Allie.

"But we're finally getting along!" I protested. "That's why I was late today! I was helping her clean out the tank!"

"WHAT?" Allie and Tamiko yelled at the same time.

"I'd do anything for my sister," I said, kind of joking.

"Just leave it be," said Tamiko. "It will all come out sooner or later, and it's not your problem."

"Yes, it *is* her problem if she's part of the cover-up. It's as good as lying to them herself," said Allie.

We were all quiet for a minute as we cleaned.

"Do you think she'll start hanging out with us again now?" asked Allie. She and Isabel had always gotten along well.

I pressed my lips together. "Ummm . . ."

"Hi, girls!" said Mrs. Shear as she breezed in from

the back office, looking all around the shop as she entered. Then she stopped in her tracks. "Oh no! Didn't anyone come in today?"

"We were packed half an hour ago . . . ," said Allie in confusion.

"There was a line out the door!" added Tamiko.

But I understood what she meant. "We cleaned up!" I said.

Mrs. Shear clapped her hand over her mouth in surprise; then she dropped it. "Wonderful work, girls! It looks like new in here!"

"It's amazing what a little music can do!" said Tamiko.

"And some teamwork!" added Allie.

"Great job. Thank you all so much. And, Sierra, Allie tells me you're getting some exciting visitors this week," said Mrs. Shear.

I nodded and grinned. "Yup! I think the kittens are coming home tomorrow."

"That will be fun," she said.

"We'll come see them whenever you get them. Even if it's a school day, right, Mom?" said Allie.

"Absolutely," said Mrs. Shear as she headed back to her office to reply to e-mails.

"And if you guys haven't told your parents about the snake by then, maybe I will!" said Allie so defiantly that I couldn't tell if she was joking or not.

"You wouldn't!" I cried.

"Just watch me, Sprinkle Squad sister!"

CHAPTER FOUR

JUST LIKE OLD TIMES

I could hardly sit still in school the next day. It felt like waiting for Christmas! Every time I started to focus, my mind would roam to the kittens and whether they'd pass their health tests and come home that afternoon.

At lunch Tamiko and I video-chatted with Allie to let her know we hadn't had any news on the cats yet. Allie couldn't wait to see them either.

Our lunch was so disgusting that day. It was what we had nicknamed "the Burritos of Sadness," when the lunch workers chopped up all the leftovers from the previous week and rolled them into big tortillas and called them burritos. Allie used her phone to show us her lunch at her beautiful new school. She was having pad thai and summer rolls with lemon iced tea. Not fair!

Right as we hung up, I spied Isa across the cafeteria. She was with some of her friends—intense soccer-playing boys. She always acted like a tough guy when she was with them. I smiled and waved at her, but she only slightly tipped her chin at me in reply, then turned to roughhouse with one of the boys. Her coolness cut like a dagger into my chest, and my smile disappeared. I had thought that we were friends again! What was the deal?

By the end of the school day, my hurt had blossomed into anger. Here I was, keeping Isabel's secret for her, helping her with her creepy snake, and she didn't even have the decency to wave back at me, her identical twin, at school? The nerve!

My mood perked up, though, when I got a text from my mom right at dismissal. The kittens are coming home today! 5:00 PM! it said.

"Woo-hoo!" I cheered, and pumped my fist into the air. Everyone at my student council meeting turned to stare at me.

"Sorry," I whispered. I quickly texted Miko and Allie; then I put my phone away and concentrated on the issues for a good ten minutes. But of course my mind floated back to the kitties, and the rest of the meeting was an agony of counting the minutes until I could leave.

At four o'clock I sprang out of my seat in the cafeteria and dashed to catch the next bus home. Checking my phone as I racewalked to the pickup spot at the curb, I saw that Allie and Tamiko had both replied that they'd be at my house by five thirty.

At home I tore around, cleaning up. Our house was always messy, but with friends coming over and the new arrivals due, I wanted things to look as good as possible. I did the breakfast dishes, recycled the papers, made my bed and my parents' bed, and straightened all the cushions and pillows in the living room. I turned on all the lights and made myself a snack of avocado toast, since I was starving after not eating much of my Burrito of Sadness. Right as I was squeezing lemon over the mashed avocado, I heard a noise behind me.

Whipping around in surprise, I saw that it was Isa. "How long have you been home?" I asked.

She shrugged, leaning in the doorway. "An hour?"

"What have you been doing?"

"Working on my science project," she said.

"Creepy. I didn't even know you were here." I turned my back on her and poured myself an ice water. I didn't offer her anything, which was unlike me, but I was mad about her ignoring me at lunch.

Bringing my plate and glass to the kitchen table, I avoided looking at her. She kept standing in the doorway.

Finally I couldn't take it anymore. "Are you just going to keep standing there watching me eat?" I exploded. I was annoyed with her from my head to my toes.

"Jeez, calm down," she said. "I'm just trying to decide what I want to eat." She crossed the room to look in the cabinets.

Now that my anger was out in the open, I decided to let her have it. "Why is it that you can't even bring yourself to say hello to me at school? Even strangers will wave back at people who smile and wave at them!"

She shrugged and kept looking in the cabinets.

"I thought we were Team P again." It was embarrassing to admit my feelings, but I had to. I was that mad.

She turned around with a smirk. "Why?"

Indignantly I said, "Um, *hello*? 'Cause I helped you with the snake and everything? And most of all, because I didn't tell Mom and Dad about her! And I could have. I should have! And you're all 'Thanks, Sisi.'" I mimicked her and then wedged a bite of the toast into my mouth and sat there, chewing furiously.

Isabel laughed. "Just because I asked for your help doesn't make us sisters for life again. We're so different. You're Little Miss Helpful, the always perfect pretty-in-pink princess, the good girl! It's *gross*. Imagine living with someone like that, who's always trying to please everyone."

My blood went cold and I dropped my toast onto my plate. "Is that what you really think of me?"

She folded her arms defiantly. "Yup!"

I stood. "Well, what about *you*, Little Miss Disagreeable, always cranky, 'no one can make me smile,' with all your weird new friends, and joining the boys' soccer team, and getting a pet snake!"

"What*ever*," said Isabel, shaking her head dismissively. She stormed out of the kitchen.

My heart was racing as I sat back down at the table. I wasn't even hungry anymore. I was upset by what I'd said to Isabel, but even more by what she'd said about me. Was it true that I was a suck-up? A princess? Little Miss Helpful? That I'd do anything to get people to like me? Isa had made me feel awful about myself.

Just then the door handle from the garage jiggled, and there was a muffled knocking. I hopped up to open the door.

"Hello?" I said before I opened it.

"Isa? It's me! Open up! My hands are full!" It was my dad.

"It's Sierra," I said, opening the door.

"Oh, sorry, *mi amor*. Here we are!" he cried, hoisting a large cardboard box through the doorway. It was covered in an old, clean towel, I guess to keep the kittens from escaping. My mom was behind him, carrying some cat supplies—a bag of litter and a litter box, a bag of dry adult cat food, and a shopping bag with some cans.

My anger at Isa melted away for the moment, and my heart swelled with excitement.

"Kittens!" I sighed. "Oh, Papi, I can't wait!" I reached to take some packages from my mom.

"*Gracias*, love," she said.

49

My dad hustled the box into the living room and placed it on the floor by the big sofa. My mom put down her packages in the kitchen, and we followed my dad.

"Where's your sister?" asked my dad.

I pointed upstairs.

"Could you please go tell her we're all here? I'll wait for you both before I open the box."

I could hear tiny meows coming from under the towel; I didn't think I could take the suspense. I was dying to see them, but I really did not want to go get Isa. Right then I didn't care if I ever saw her again. But we didn't disobey my parents at our house. Or at least, Isabel hadn't ever before, and I still wouldn't.

Reluctantly I stood and trudged upstairs. I crossed the landing and knocked on her door. There was no reply.

I knocked again. "Cats are here," I said dully.

Still no reply. She was probably in her closet and couldn't hear me. Gently I pushed open the door, and spied Isabel sprawled on her bed, face-down.

"Isa?"

"Go away," she grumbled.

"The cats are here. Dad says to come down."

"I don't care," she said.

I paused. *What now?*

"Come on. He's waiting for us both before he even lets them out. I don't want him to get annoyed. Let's go."

"Go ahead," she said.

I took one last look at her. "Fine. But you're the one who's going to get in trouble for disobeying, not me. Mom and Dad are waiting for you."

"Do you really think I care?" she asked, raising her tearstained face to me at last.

I was shocked to see her crying, and it melted my anger a tiny bit. Isa rarely cried. I didn't know what to say, so I just stood there awkwardly for a minute. Inside, my head swirled all the insults about me being Little Miss Helpful, which didn't exactly make me want to comfort her right then. But still, a little part of me did feel bad, and I couldn't help but wonder if I was partially guilty for Isabel's tears.

After a moment I shrugged.

"I bet they're pretty cute?" I said hopefully. "Just

come down for a little bit. It wouldn't hurt to snuggle them for a minute, would it?"

There was a pause, and then Isabel said, "Fine. But I'm going to wash my face first. Tell them I was asleep and I'm coming."

Another lie? Nope. If we were going to be brutally honest with each other, then I was done lying for her.

"I'll just tell them you're coming," I said. And I turned and went back downstairs.

A moment later we were all there, and my dad lifted the towel. "Ta-da!" he cried, and the kittens all started clamoring to get out. The mama cat hopped out first and cased the room, sniffing at everything and roaming behind and underneath all the furniture. My mom put out a dish with water and a dish with dry food for her, and the cat smelled it twice before she settled in to eat, placing her front paws together as she did.

The kittens, though, were wild and spastic. Isa and I sat on the rug with my parents, and we pushed aside the coffee table, creating a large central area bounded by our legs. As the kittens reached the perimeter and tried to escape, we'd gently lift them and put them back into the middle. Their little claws were like needles through the thin fabric of my pants, and I winced and laughed every time one tried to scale my leg like a little mountaineer.

Each kitten looked different from the others, though they were all tiny, with oversize heads, short skinny tails, and super-fluffy fur. One kitten had an orange back with a mostly white face and chest; one had pale orange and white stripes all over; and the other was darker, almost solidly orange, with a white triangle on its chest. The mom also had orange and white stripes, and big white paws.

"They're little Creamsicle fluffballs!" I cooed.

Isabel seemed amused by them, but she was acting standoffish, almost as if she didn't *want* to like them.

I wanted to say, "I guess now that you're a snake person, you can't find kittens cute, right?"

But I didn't.

I kept picking up the kittens and snuggling them until they struggled to get away. Then I'd scoop up another one. "They don't want me to hold them! They keep running away!" I said.

"Keep trying. It's good to handle them," said my mom. "It helps to socialize them."

"Why are their ears like that?" asked Isabel. The kittens' ears were all sort of small and folded in.

"Because they're still so young," said my dad. "Their ears will get bigger and open up in another week or two. They're practically newborns."

"Wait, so how old are they now?" I asked.

"We think about six weeks," said my dad.

"Are they boys or girls?" asked Isabel.

"Actually, we can't tell yet," said my mom. "They have to be around eight weeks old for us to know for sure."

"Huh," I said. "Are you sisters or brothers?" I leaned in and asked them in baby talk.

"Does it matter?" laughed my dad. "They don't care. They'll still play together and have fun and snuggle up either way."

I thought about it, and then I shrugged. "I guess you're right."

Suddenly the doorbell rang. "It's Tamiko and Allie!" I said. "I'll get it." I hopped up, and my family closed the circle to cover for where I'd been. I wondered how Isa would treat Tamiko and Allie.

I flung open the door. *"Chicas!"* I cried. "Wait till you see!"

They put down the bags they were carrying and scurried across the living room to where my family sat and the kittens were waiting.

"OMG!" cried Allie, putting her hands to the sides of her face, almost as if the kittens' cuteness pained her.

"Seriously? These are ridiculous!" said Tamiko. "Hi, Isabel! Hi, Drs. Perez!"

"Hi, girls!" my parents greeted my friends. Isabel didn't say anything, but she scooted over to make room for the three of us to join the circle.

"Where's the mommy cat?" asked Allie.

"Up there," said my dad, pointing to the back of the sofa, where the cat had curled up and fallen fast asleep.

Tamiko laughed. "She sure doesn't seem too concerned about us holding her babies!"

My mom smiled. "She's been so vigilant for so long. Mama cats get tired from all the work. They have to nurse the cats and herd them so that they don't wander off. Then the moms are always licking them clean, and their licking motion helps the babies go to the bathroom, which they can't even do on their own. When the kittens get to an age when they don't need their mama to hover over them, sometimes the moms need a break. She must trust us and feel comfortable here already if she's gone off to sleep like that. She needs the rest."

"Poor thing," said Allie. "That sounds like a lot of work." She looked back at the kittens. "Is it okay if we touch them or pick them up?"

"Sure," said my dad. He snagged one of the kittens and offered it to Allie.

"Oh! What a little cutie!" she said as she snuggled the kitten against her chest. "I wish I could have another cat."

"I wish I could have *one*," I said quietly.

My mom put her hands in the air. "Remember, people. This is just temporary! These cats need forever homes!"

I sighed and caught Allie's eye. She raised her eyebrows at me, and I knew she was asking about Naga. I gave a tiny shake of my head to let her know that my parents still didn't know. Allie rolled her eyes.

Tamiko saw the look and gushed, "Hey! Amber says Gizmo is doing great!" Amber was our friend who had adopted the abandoned shih tzu that we'd fostered.

"I know!" I said. "She showed me a photo this morning at school. He's all groomed and filled out and handsome now."

"That pup was a fighter," said my dad, shaking his head in admiration. "We didn't think he'd make it at first, he was so skinny and sick."

"Remember Roman, Dad? Isa and I were just talking about him. . . ."

"He's still a client of ours!" said my mom happily. "We get to see him at least once a year. He's doing great! His name is Paco now."

"You're so lucky. We fall in love with all these animals for a few days, and then we never see them again!" I said.

Isabel spoke up. "Yeah. You're with pets all day, so you don't realize what it's like. We foster these guys, and then they're gone!"

My parents exchanged a look, and my mom sighed. "I know. Maybe when you're in high school we can get something low-maintenance and easy and you girls can be in charge of it."

I glanced at Allie, then looked quickly away. *Please don't say anything, please don't say anything,* I pleaded silently.

Tamiko interrupted with a cheery, "Hey, so what are y'all naming these critters?"

Isabel and I looked at each other. We always picked names together for the animals that stayed with us, even though their names usually changed once they were gone. (Gizmo had been "Chichi" before Amber adopted him.) Usually we'd each write three names down on scraps of paper. Then we'd pull the name or names out of a dish, and that would be that. It was the only fair way. The Team P way.

But today my dad had another idea. "Why don't each of *you* name a cat? Here." He handed the dark orange one to Isabel, the mostly white one to me, and the light orange one to Allie, and he gestured to the mama cat for Tamiko.

I looked down at the white one in my lap and thought for a second. Then I said, "Marshmallow."

Allie smiled at hers and said, "Butterscotch."

Tamiko grinned and said, "Honey."

We all looked at Isa expectantly. Would she play along with us or go totally rogue and name hers "Spike"?

"Cinnamon," she said, and we all breathed a sigh of relief. "But I'll call her '*Mon*ster' as a nickname. Get it? 'Mon' from 'Cinna*mon*'! My little monster!"

"Oh, Isa!" said Allie, laughing. "Always the rene-gade!"

"Hey, the gift!" said Tamiko, hopping up and scurrying to their bags by the door. "We bought this for you guys on the way over."

Tamiko and Allie presented me with a small plastic bag. I opened it and inside found the toy that Allie's cat, Diana, loved best—a telescoping wand with a long ribbon on it that pulled a little tuft of feathers and streamers around.

"We used to play for hours with Diana with one of these, and she loved it," said Allie.

"I remember! Thank you so much!" I looked at Isa and spontaneously held the toy out to her. "Here. You try it first," I said.

Isabel hesitated, but then took it from me and extended the handle. She dangled the toy in front of Marshmallow, and she (or he?) instantly pounced on it, rolled onto her back, held it in her front paws, and scrabbled at it with her rear paws.

Cinnamon bounded over to see what was up, and she got in on the act too. She stood on her hind legs, opened her front paws wide, and dive-bombed

Marshmallow. We all cracked up, watching the kitten antics. Every time Isabel could get the toy free, she'd zoom it around, and the kittens would chase and pounce and wrestle.

"It's funny how they play together," said Allie.

"They remind me of you two when you were little!" my mom said to me and Isabel.

"Totally!" agreed my dad. "You'd tumble all over the place, wrestling over things and getting into mischief, and then we'd find you both exhausted, curled up together, fast asleep."

"Awwww!" teased Tamiko.

I stole a glance at Isabel to see her reaction. She was looking down and jerking the toy around, but she was smiling. *Sisters forever,* I thought.

After a bit, my parents went to start dinner, and Isabel wandered off upstairs. Tamiko found a cardboard box in our garage and with a box cutter and some packing tape quickly created a play space for the kittens, complete with ramps, different levels, and a little hiding area.

When it was finished, we all oohed and aahed over it. I caught myself about to say "It's just like Naga's cave!" but luckily I didn't.

My friends had to go by six thirty. They were reluctant to leave, and I was sad to see them go. Hanging out with the three of us and Isa—even for that brief time—had felt like the old days, when things had been happier and less complicated at my house.

Little did I know how much more complicated things would get!

CHAPTER FIVE

KITTEN CAFÉ—FOR A DAY!

The week passed in a blur of after-school activities and kitten fur. I spent every free moment I had at home playing with the kitties (to the harm of my homework). During the school day and workday, when the cats were home alone, they were kept closed up in the kitchen with their food (wet for the kittens, dry for the mom), water, and litter box. When Isa or I got home after school, our job was to release them into the living room and play with them for a while.

It was funny how the cats' personalities wound up being just like the people who'd named them. Honey, the mama cat, was inquisitive and into everything. I kept finding her sleeping in new and more outrageous places every day, like in the linen closet, in a potted plant, and once, when she had somehow gotten into the garage, on the hood of my parents' car. She was definitely sporting Tamiko's flair and originality.

Butterscotch was just like Allie: she was sweet and cuddly and mellow. Marshmallow was, *ahem*, everywhere and into everything. Anytime another kitten would start playing with something or checking something out, Marshmallow would race over and poke her nose in. All week as I watched Marshy, I thought about Isabel's criticisms of me, and that made me see myself in a new (not entirely positive) light. Why *did* I sign up to help with everything? Why *did* I need to be helping and volunteering all the time, even if it compromised my schoolwork? Why *couldn't* I say no to anyone? The way she'd said it had been mean, but it did make me think.

As for Cinnamon, "Monster" was a good nickname. She was tough and brave, and she was the one always venturing farther and farther away from "home"—her siblings, her play space, and her mom. Maybe *that* was Isa's jam. She was ready to try things away from our little family.

It just hurt that I was being left behind.

I wondered how Marshmallow and Butterscotch felt. They did nothing but play with each other all day. No sibling problems here.

On Sunday I needed to be half an hour early to work at Molly's Ice Cream to make up for the week before, so I conscientiously finished all my extra-curricular work and homework on Saturday. I had to admit that it felt amazing to wake up Sunday morning without a care in the world! After church and brunch, my parents went to see an emergency patient and check on the renovations. They said they wouldn't be home until six and they'd bring home pizza for an easy dinner. I was in charge of baby-sitting the kitties until it was time for me to leave at eleven forty-five. Then Isa would take over until our parents got home.

I was dressed and ready to go to work by eleven thirty, and just as I was pulling on my shoes, I heard a muffled scream from upstairs.

"Isa?" I called.

"Sierra! Come quick!" Isabel's voice sounded far away, but I could hear the panic in it.

I glanced at the kittens, and they seemed like

they'd be okay for a minute alone, so I bounded up the stairs, two at a time.

Isabel's door was closed, so I pushed it open and poked my head in. Isabel was pale and shaking a little bit.

"Come in and close the door. Quick!" she said.

I did as I was told while asking, "What's up?"

Isabel looked at me in horror. "Naga's missing!"

"What?" My mouth formed an O of shock as my eyes darted all around the room. "Is she in here?"

Isabel shrugged miserably as she cast her eyes all over. "I don't know. I left my bedroom door open when I went to take my shower. I guess I didn't put the books back properly after I cleaned her tank earlier, and she pushed her way out. She might be here or . . ."

"OMG, the kittens! Could she have gone downstairs?" Francie's word—"constrictor"—passed through my mind.

"I don't know!"

Scared and frustrated, I glanced at my phone. It read 11:35.

"Isa, I am so sorry, but I have to go. I have to leave for work in the next ten minutes."

Isabel glared at me. "Fine! So when I need help, I don't count? Allie and Tamiko come first?"

I sighed. "Isabel, it's my job. I was late last week because I *was* helping you with the tank, and now I'm in trouble. I can't be late again or I'll be fired."

"What am I going to do? I can't watch the kittens and look for Naga at the same time. And what if Mom and Dad come home before I find her?"

"Isa, you have to tell them either way. This has gone on too long. If you don't tell Mom and Dad about Naga tonight, I'm telling them."

Isabel looked downcast. "You know what? I don't really want to keep her anymore," she said in a small voice. "She's too much work. Also . . . she's cool and all . . . but . . . she's not that cuddly."

I nodded sadly at Isabel. "I'm sorry."

"The kittens made me realize . . ."

I nodded again. "I know."

"I just need to find her another home, I think," she said.

"I'm sure Mami and Papi could help you find her a home."

"I guess," she said quietly.

I took a deep breath, and then, thinking of the cat

cafés in Japan that Tamiko had told us about, I blurted, "I'm going to take the kittens to work with me. Just let me find a box, and I'll leave with them. Then you can look for Naga without any distractions."

Isa looked up gratefully. "Really?" she said. And then, "Wait. Do you think that's a good idea?"

I was actually getting enthused by the idea the more I thought about it.

"Yes! We need to find homes for the kitties, right? Plus, Mom said they need lots of handling to socialize them—which they're not getting enough of here—*and* it solves our Naga problem. I'm doing it!" I finished confidently. "As soon as you find Naga, you can come to Molly's and pick them up, and don't tell Mom or Dad. Okay?"

"O-kaaaay?" said Isabel skeptically, but I was already committed.

"Let's just pinky promise to keep each other's secrets for now. Deal?"

Isabel nodded and stuck out her pinky for me to hook with mine. "Deal," she said solemnly as we shook on it with our pinkies. For a second I felt like we were five again, or eight, or even eleven, when we'd still been partners in crime.

I jogged down the stairs and popped into the garage to find a spare box. Unsurprisingly, given the state of our garage, the box that the cats had arrived in was still there. I grabbed it and the towel that was folded inside, and I went into the living room to bundle the kittens into the box. I'd leave Honey behind. She was too big to sit in a box for an hour, and anyway, I figured she could outrun Naga if need be. Or at least I hoped she could.

I put the box into an old laundry cart we had and added a water bowl and some food, then called Tamiko to tell her my plan. She thought it was a "killer" idea and offered to meet me outside Molly's in fifteen minutes or so. I was relieved that she didn't think I was crazy.

I set out for Molly's, walking as fast as I could, avoiding the bumps and cracks in the sidewalk as I pushed the laundry cart. I had sweet, furry precious cargo, after all!

I rounded the corner and spied Tamiko waiting for me under the blue-and-cream-striped awning of Molly's. She saw me and darted over to say hi.

"Like I said, animal cafés are all the rage in Japan. Since we can't charge an entry fee like they do there, we'll just have to charge a little extra 'playing fee' for people who want to sit with the kittens and play with them. Right?"

I nodded, suddenly nervous. Tamiko had a tendency to come up with marketing and publicity ideas for Molly's that she thought were great but that Mrs. Shear found kind of hasty and half-baked. I worried this might fall into that category. (Ha-ha. Get it? "Cat"-egory?) I gulped when we reached the door, and Tamiko held it for me so that I could wheel in the kitten cart.

As luck would have it (or not), Mrs. Shear was standing right inside the door, straightening some menus. Noontime was always pretty quiet at Molly's, I'd noticed. The real daytime rush was after lunch and then again after beach time, in season.

"Girls! Hi! You're here so early today! I just sent Allie to the grocery store to buy some sugar for my Saint Louis Cake ice cream," she said cheerfully. "What's in the cart?"

Tamiko took center stage, explaining the idea but talking a mile a minute. "See, we have some kittens that need to be adopted, and you know about cat cafés, right? In Japan? And so we thought it would be so cool to do that here? And we can put it up on social media to get people in, and it would be really good publicity, and maybe we could donate some of the fees to the animal shelter. . . ." Tamiko hadn't even taken a breath. I already knew the plan, and even *I* was confused!

Mrs. Shear shook her head as if to clear it. "Okay, wait, slow down. *What?*"

I jumped in and explained about the pet cafés in detail. Mrs. Shear folded her arms across her chest, leaned back against the counter, and listened. Then Tamiko interjected again, saying, "We thought it would be cool to do it here. Today. Since Sierra's watching these kittens."

It was becoming clear that Mrs. Shear not only didn't love the idea but was actually pretty uncomfortable with it.

"Gosh, girls. I wish you'd asked me first. There are really strict health code rules—state and local— about pets not being allowed in places that sell or serve food. I would lose my license if I were caught with animals in here." She was shaking her head.

I was crestfallen, but Tamiko was thinking on her feet. "Well," she said, "it's so beautiful today that maybe we could move a couple of tables outside and set something up out there? It's worth a try. Even if only for an hour or so, right, Sierra?"

I nodded along with her. "Yeah!"

"Are your parents okay with this plan?" asked Mrs. Shear.

I was really getting sick of lying. I wanted to tell the truth, but I also wanted to protect Isabel. And I wanted to make Tamiko happy.

"Well," I said, "they told me how important it was to handle and socialize the kittens."

There. It wasn't a lie.

Mrs. Shear tapped her chin, thinking. "Hmm. It might work. One of you would need to stay out there with the cats, though. If we get a rush inside . . ."

"We work really well as a team. I think we can make this work," said Tamiko, not wanting Mrs. Shear to discuss every possible thing that could go wrong. "If it's a total fail, we'll call Isabel and tell her to come get the kittens earlier than planned. Okay?"

Allie appeared then. "Hey! What's in the box?" she asked.

Her mom turned to her and smiled wryly. "Looks like we're hosting a kitten café here today," she said.

"No way! You have the cats in there?" she said, trying to peer into the box. "Oh, Mom, you won't believe how cute they are. Like I told you, they remind me so much of Diana when she was a baby!"

"It certainly is lucky that you girls were early today. Now you can use the extra time to get set up," said Mrs. Shear, smiling.

I realized that Allie hadn't told her I was late the week before. I reached over and squeezed Allie's hand, and she understood, squeezing back.

"Thanks," I whispered.

"Sometimes you do things for sisters," Allie whispered back.

Tamiko had already propped open the door and was moving some chairs outside.

"Should we take this table together?" I asked Allie, and so we did.

Soon all the furniture we needed was outside, and Tamiko had arranged it so that people could sit and watch the kittens.

"I don't have a sidewalk permit," said Mrs. Shear anxiously.

Tamiko said, "If you get a bucket and a mop and put them inside the door, we can just say we moved

72

everything outside because . . . someone threw up and we needed to clean the floor!"

Mrs. Shear laughed and made a disgusted face, but she shook her head. "No. I won't lie. I don't think that the inspector will come here during this particular hour on a Sunday."

"Now, we need someone to stay out here with the kitties," said Tamiko. "Also, I'll make a sign so people know they're up for adoption. Allie, do you still have that big roll of white bakery paper?"

"Yup. It's in the storage closet off the kitchen. Hello, Scotchy!" she said, lifting the towel off the box and peeking her head in.

"Allie, I think *you* should be the one to sit out here with the cats," I said, still feeling grateful to her for covering for me. Sitting with the cats would be fun for her. "Tamiko and I will handle everything inside."

I helped Allie get settled with the kitties, making sure we had a barrier set up so that they couldn't get too far. I set up water bowls for them and made a little bed out of the towel in case they needed to take a nap. Then I went in to help Tamiko do the signs. Mrs. Shear stayed behind the counter until we were ready to take over our real job—serving ice cream.

Soon we had three signs saying ADOPT A KITTY! and two saying KITTEN CAFÉ: PAY TO PLAY! $5. ALL DONATIONS GO TO THE BAYVILLE ANIMAL SHELTER. I brought Allie a clean ice cream pint container to use for collecting money, and a minute later she had three people gathered around her, all eager to play with the kitties.

Tamiko and I assumed our spots behind the counter and watched through the big plate-glass window as tons of people stopped to say hi, check out the kittens, and come in for ice cream. Whether they were coming in anyway or whether the cats lured them in, it was hard to say, but business was good. Tamiko took a break during a lull and snapped pics of the kittens—a few with adorable little kid customers with their parents holding them—and posted them on social media with all kinds of hashtags.

Allie had each kitten settled in a chair outside with a customer, Tamiko was scrolling through the social feeds for Molly's to see how people were reacting to the kitten posts, Mrs. Shear was in the back in her office doing paperwork, and I had texted Isa to come—whether she'd found Naga or not—in ten minutes. Everything seemed to be going perfectly, when the shop bell jingled and in walked two unexpected customers: my parents.

CHAPTER SIX

I'M SIERRA THE SNITCH

"Are those kittens out there?" my mother stage-whispered indignantly as she approached the counter.

My father was giving me the hairy eyeball.

"Sierra, why don't you go on break? I'll cover," said Tamiko, her eyes wide.

"Thanks," I said gratefully, gulping. "What are you guys doing here?" I asked my parents sweetly.

"We thought it would be nice to come see you at work and have a Sunday treat. We had no idea what we'd find!" said my dad sternly.

My mother steered me outside and a little past the cat café, out of earshot, and I braced myself for the coming storm.

"Sierra, what are you thinking, taking these kittens out of our house? It's so dangerous for them! They're still so young! We don't even let them out of the kitchen when we're not home!"

"Mami! I was in a pinch. I couldn't watch them— and anyway, you said they need to be handled by people to get them socialized." I was rambling, grasping at straws, but I couldn't really think straight. I'd never considered that I might get caught.

"Yes, but handled by people who know what they're doing, in a safe indoor space. Not every random person walking down the street!" protested my mom.

"What about Isabel? Had she left the house?" asked my father, his brow furrowed.

I sighed heavily. I was going to have to come clean, for both or us. "Isa couldn't watch the kittens, and I couldn't leave them there alone because . . ." I cringed, dreading divulging the information that would cause me pain in more ways than one.

My parents looked at me expectantly.

"*¿Si?*" prompted my mom.

I took a deep breath. "Because Isa has a pet snake and it got loose in the house and she had to find it. So we couldn't leave the kittens there unattended."

"What?!?" cried my father. "There's a *snake* in my own house, and I didn't even know it? Sierra! This is serious! What kind of snake?!"

"It's—it's a corn snake!" I stammered.

"How can you be sure, Sierra? Corn snakes look just like copperheads, which are highly venomous and dangerous!" said my mom.

"I . . . uh . . . the girl told her . . ."

"And who exactly is this girl?" asked my dad.

"Uh . . . Francie?" I said, realizing that I knew exactly zero about Francie, or about Naga's origins.

My parents looked at each other, their mouths in matching grim lines. Suddenly I realized how serious this Naga business was.

"We might have to call animal control," said my mom.

"Isa should get out of that house," said my dad. He sprang into action, his fingers flying over his phone screen as he called home. He stared at me with the phone to his ear, waiting and waiting.

"No answer," he said, stabbing at the screen with his thumb to disconnect the call.

"Try her cell," I suggested. "She might be on her way here now."

"If she wasn't bitten by a copperhead!" scolded my mom.

My dad punched in Isabel's cell number and put the phone to his ear. Just as he was about to hang up, Isabel answered, while at the same moment she rounded the corner right in front of us.

"Hello?" she was saying.

My dad looked at her and hung up the phone.

Isabel's eyes grew wide, and she looked to me to read the situation.

"They know," I said flatly. "We're in trouble."

"Isa! Did you find the snake?" asked my mom urgently.

Isabel nodded, her face a mask of shock.

My parents both breathed a sigh of relief. "It didn't bite you, did it?" asked my dad.

Isabel shook her head. "Corn snakes don't bite."

My dad huffed in aggravation. "Assuming it *is* a corn snake. Let's go," he said.

He marched us back up the block to the cat café setup. He nicely told Allie to wrap it up. "The kittens are probably tired," he said, "so we should get them home." He directed me to take down the cat signs and for me and Isabel to help put the furniture back

79

while he and my mom went in to say hi and explain everything to Mrs. Shear.

Once we were alone outside, I whispered to Isa, "I'm sorry, but I had to tell them!"

She wouldn't even look at me.

"Isa! It's not my fault! I told you that you should have told them from the beginning!"

Allie watched us with wide eyes but didn't say anything. She was always fascinated by the sister thing because she only had her little brother, Tanner.

"Isa! Say something!"

Nothing but silence.

We quickly put the furniture back, all without a word from Isabel, and then we went back outside. Allie had wrapped up the play sessions by then and was counting the money. We'd made fifty dollars in an hour! That was at least a silver lining. It would all be donated to the animal shelter.

Shortly my parents came out with Mrs. Shear, chatting and friendly. It gave me a false sense for the moment that they weren't really mad at us, but my dad's eyes were hard when they met mine. Eeek!

"I think we all learned something today," Mrs. Shear said, looking at me. I could tell from her face that my parents had told her we'd cooked up this plan without their permission. I could also tell she was disappointed in me.

I looked down, then looked up and met her eyes. "I'm sorry," I said.

"I can take a lot of things, but not lying," said Mrs. Shear. "Lying always makes it worse, Sierra."

Allie looked at me like she wanted to help. "Well, on a happy note, we made fifty dollars for the animal shelter."

"Wow. That's wonderful!" said my mom. "Doing acts of kindness is always a good thing."

"Maybe after we all think about it, there's a way to do this the right way," said Mrs. Shear. "As long as everyone is on board."

"I'm sure the shelter would love to send their adoption van over," said my mom, sipping her shake. "We can help coordinate that."

"The one with all the little habitats inside, with the cats and dogs for adoption?" asked Allie.

My mom nodded. "That's the one. They're always looking for venues to get the needy animals in front of people."

"Great idea. Then we wouldn't have to have the

animals inside the shop or our furniture out on the pavement. Allie, why don't you look into that?" suggested Mrs. Shear.

Allie nodded.

"I'll check into the ordinances with the town and figure out if we can have it here again, all on the up-and-up," Mrs. Shear added.

"We're dropping Isa and the kittens at home and then heading back to the clinic," said Mom. "Sierra, we'll see you straightaway when you're finished here, right?"

I nodded.

"We'll talk when we all get home," added my mom.

My parents and Isabel wheeled away the laundry cart with the box full of kittens.

I felt so guilty about having betrayed Isabel and the fact that she had to face the wrath of my parents alone. But at the same time I was soooo relieved to not have to deal with them until later, when they'd hopefully cooled off a bit.

We went back inside to work. Unfortunately, Tamiko's social media blitz had been a little too successful. Seven more people stopped by to see the kittens, and we had to explain that they'd left for the day. We also said we hoped to have another event soon.

"But they should be back soon. We'll post in advance if so. Meanwhile, wouldn't you love a kitten sundae to ease your disappointment?" Tamiko asked.

She'd invented a kitten sundae, just as Allie had predicted, and it was supercute: a huge scoop of ice cream in a dish, with two blue M&M's for eyes, a red M&M for a nose, two halves of a wafer for ears, and chocolate syrup from a squirt bottle to create three whiskers on either side of the nose.

"Cute idea, Miko," I'd said enthusiastically when I saw it.

"It would be cool to charge a little extra for these and put the balance in a jar for the animal shelter."

"I like that idea, but I think we've had enough innovation for the day," I said wearily.

During a lull I went to the bathroom and texted Isabel.

I'M SO SORRY, I wrote, and pressed send.

No response.

ARE U MAD AT ME? I wrote.

No response.

DID THEY YELL THE WHOLE WAY HOME?

Still no response.

And finally, WILL YOU EVER FORGIVE ME?

But there was still no reply from her when I'd finished work and had said my good-byes to head home at the end of the day. Allie and Tamiko promised to stay near their phones in case I needed them, and Allie hugged me fiercely.

"I am trying really hard not to say 'I told you so,'" said Allie into my shoulder.

"Then don't say it!" I joked. "But thanks for not telling your mom I was late last week."

"And I forgive you for not taking my advice and telling your parents about Naga earlier!" Allie said, giggling.

Tamiko rolled her eyes. "See, I told you it would all work out!"

"Well," I said, "we don't really know how it will work out." I took a deep breath. "Wish me luck, sisters. It's time to face the music."

For the first time ever, I dreaded going home.

CHAPTER SEVEN

PIZZA AND PUNISHMENT

I beat my parents home by ten minutes. The kittens were locked in the kitchen, so my first stop was to see if Isa was even home. Her door was closed and she didn't answer when I knocked. When I tried the handle, it wouldn't turn. We didn't have locks on our doors, so that meant that she had her desk chair wedged under the doorknob. If *that* was the case, I knew better than to keep trying.

Back in my room I took a minute to Google "copperhead snake" and "corn snake." Um, yeah. They did look alike. I shivered.

"Hello!" my mom called from downstairs. I heard the door to the garage slam.

"Girls!" called my dad.

I steeled myself and called back, "Coming!" Then I stopped by Isa's room and knocked softly again.

"Isabel! They're back. You have to come."

I wasn't waiting to see if she'd come. I slowly walked down the stairs and into the kitchen. There was a large pizza box sitting on top of the stove. I didn't dare ask if they'd bought garlic knots, too, which were Isa's and my favorite thing, and something my parents wouldn't always get for us. I was pretty sure they weren't feeling too kindly toward us right about then.

"Get a slice of pizza and a drink, and let's all meet in the dining room," directed my dad.

I turned and saw that Isabel had materialized in the doorway. I looked away. Now I was mad. I was in big trouble, and this was all her fault! If she hadn't had the stupid snake in the first place, or if she'd at least told my parents about it, I never would have had to cover for her or take the kittens to work, and we never would have gotten into this situation.

I grabbed a slice, poured myself some ice water, and stalked into the living room, not meeting anyone's eye.

My dad had left the door open between the

rooms, and the kittens started to migrate into the dining room after us. Soon Marshmallow and Cinnamon were tussling on the floor.

I sat in a chair on my own; I didn't want to sit next to anyone on the couch. I didn't even wait for everyone to be served before I started eating. I just gnashed into my slice and started chewing, watching the cats play. Right then I was wishing I were a cat. I bet Honey never yelled at her kittens. I bet Cinnamon never brought home something inappropriate and made Marshmallow lie about it!

My dad joined me, and we sat in silence and chewed, and then my mom and Isabel arrived, my mom sitting next to my dad and Isabel opposite me.

My mom sighed heavily, then bit into her pizza.

My dad finished his slice and cleared his throat.

There was only the sound of chewing for a few seconds.

Luckily, just then Cinnamon came flying off the cabinet, kamikaze-style, and landed on Marshmallow on the rug below, and we all laughed. The tension was broken, and my parents began to speak at the same time.

"You girls have broken our trust—" began my mom.

"Mami and I are very upset—" said my dad.

They each gestured for the other to continue, while Isabel and I sat there in dread.

My mom began again. "You girls have both broken our trust. Isabel, you defied our 'no pets' rule and brought an animal to live under our roof without our permission or knowledge. You did it knowingly and sneakily, and with great risk to you and the animal, and we are very angry about that."

My dad nodded and swallowed his bite of pizza. Then he took over for my mom. "And you, Sierra. You went along with Isabel's bad decision and secret-keeping, and you also made decisions on behalf of the kittens today that were not your decisions to make. You put them in danger."

They both looked at us until we met their eyes.

"I'm very disappointed in the lying," said my mom. "In both of you. How do we know that we can trust you in the future? And at a time when you're both seeking more freedom and independence! How can we trust you to tell us the truth? If you don't have truth, you don't have trust."

I could feel the redness rising in my cheeks. Allie had been right all along. We should have come clean.

I'd just been selfish because I'd liked having a secret with Isa again, feeling like partners in crime, Team P, sisters for life.

"Taking the kittens out was simply ill-considered and impulsive," said my mom. "You should have asked us first."

"And if you lie or cause us to distrust you, then the consequence is punishment," said my dad. "Both of you girls will be spending the next four Saturday mornings working at the clinic as volunteers. You'll be cleaning up after the animals, sending specimens to the lab, filing, whatever we ask of you. Do you understand?"

I nodded and snuck a sidelong glance at Isabel. She was nodding too. This was a drag—they'd be making us do the worst jobs there. ("Sending specimens to the lab" meant handling all the animal poop samples, and "cleaning up after the animals" meant mopping up the pee from the nervous visitors, and vomit and worse from the sick ones.) It would also kill my chunk of time for getting homework and extracurriculars done, which would effectively cancel my social life for the next month.

"What about soccer?" asked Isa.

My dad raised his eyebrows and looked at my mom.

"It will be on a case-by-case basis," said my mom. "We'll decide which activities you can participate in."

"Now let's talk about this snake." My dad sighed and put his empty plate on the table, then sat back and folded his arms.

I lifted my head. "Did you see it?"

My mom nodded. "I came up when we dropped Isabel off earlier. It is a corn snake. Thank goodness."

Isabel lifted her chin defiantly. "I *told* you!"

"It has to go, Isa," said my dad.

"I know!" blurted Isabel. "I don't even want her here anymore! She's more trouble than she's worth."

My mom shook her head and put her palm to her chest. "It *pains* me to hear people speak about animals like that. When you take on the responsibility of a pet . . ."

"It's for life," Isabel and I intoned at the same time. It was my mom's mantra, one we'd heard probably a thousand times.

She smiled thinly. "Well, at least we know that something is getting through."

I tried to catch Isabel's eye to smile at her, but she wouldn't look at me.

"However," said my dad, "Naga was a mistake. We never would have approved her as a family pet. I'm sorry, Isa, but it's true. I know she doesn't bite, but having a constrictor of any sort in a family home is a huge liability. Besides, what do you think she eats when she graduates from baby mice?" He squinted at Isabel.

"Grown-up mice?" she said.

He nodded. "And then?"

She shrugged.

He cleared his throat and sat forward in his seat. "Rats. Rabbits, even. Depends on how big she gets."

Isabel looked aghast. "What?"

My mom was nodding.

"Kittens?" I asked.

My dad shook his head. "That would be very rare."

"But not impossible?" I pressed.

"Naga's not an adult snake, anyway!" protested Isabel. "Why are you trying to make this all sound worse than it is?"

"Why are you yelling at me? You don't even want her, so what do you care?" I yelled.

Isabel huffed and folded her arms.

"Girls, please. Let's not fight," Mom said.

"I have some contacts that I'll be in touch with tomorrow," said my dad as he stood with his plate to go get another slice of pizza. "I don't think it will be a problem to find someone to take a healthy young corn snake. But I hate having to do it. It makes me look like a fool to be suffering from the 'accidental pet' problem in my own family." He looked at us grimly. "Vets don't make mistakes like that." He left the room.

I nearly said, "Couldn't you just lie about who it belongs to?" but I caught myself just in time. Yikes! I was in danger of turning into quite the dishonest person.

"In addition," said my mother, actually wagging her finger back and forth at the two of us. "I don't like the discord I'm seeing between you two over the past few months. Now, obviously, we can't force you to get along, but I'd like you both to make more of an effort with each other. We're only four people in this family, and if half of us aren't getting along, it really affects the whole. You are so lucky to have each other, and it breaks my heart to see you at odds."

I stared straight ahead, not even looking at Isabel.

I was sure she wasn't looking at me, either.

"Get it together, girls," said my mom. "You are sisters. Sisters for life. *¿Entienden?*"

I nodded slightly. "Yes. I understand." Out of the corner of my eye, I could see Isabel nod once.

My dad came back with the box of pizza and offered it around to everyone. So they hadn't bought garlic knots. They must really have been mad.

But then my mom said, "Andres, what did you do with the knots?"

And my dad said, "*¡Ay!* I left them in the warming bag in the car. Hang on."

Well. At least they didn't totally hate us.

I promised myself I wouldn't even try to speak to Isabel that night, but I couldn't stand having someone mad at me, especially if we were under the same roof. Especially when it was my sister. One of us had to make the first move. After I took my shower and cleaned up my room (sort of), I'd run out of things to do. I was going to go downstairs and watch a movie with my parents, but I thought it was worth trying just one more time to get Isa to talk to me.

I knocked on her door.

No reply.

I knocked again.

Nothing.

Finally I turned her door handle a tiny bit, and feeling no resistance, I opened the door. Inside, Isabel sat with her back to her closed closet door, Naga in her lap. She looked up at me scornfully and said nothing.

I closed the door and left.

Later I texted Allie and Tamiko to tell them about our punishment.

You got off easy, Allie replied.

Kinda agree, said Tamiko.

I paused. Then I typed, Isabel is still not speaking to me. Might never again.

I watched the screen to see what they would say.

Finally Allie replied, Things usually look better in the morning. Go to sleep.

And Tamiko added, What she said.

I plugged in my phone and powered down for the night. I hoped they were right.

CHAPTER EIGHT
FRIENDS AND FAMILY

The next morning Isabel was gone by the time I got downstairs. I was disappointed.

I'd awoken with a fresh outlook, just as Allie had said, and I'd been hoping to make peace. It was frustrating that Isabel had left early.

At breakfast the kitties were going to new lengths to amuse themselves. Shimmying behind the fridge and getting stuck, scaling a bath towel hanging on the laundry closet doorknob—until the towel slipped and sent the kitten cartwheeling backward across the floor.

"They're really into everything, aren't they?" I said to my mom, who was leaning against the cabinet and drinking her coffee with a faraway look on her face.

"Mmm-hmm. They remind me of you girls when you were little."

She kept saying that. I hesitated, but then I said quietly, "Mami, I miss Isa. Why does she hate me so much?"

My mom came and put her arm around me. "Oh, *mi amor*. Being your age is so tough. All you kids are trying to understand life and who you are. I think Isa is trying to figure out who she is and what she wants to be, and unlike most preteens, she has a mirror image staring back at her all the time. Imagine trying to reinvent yourself by changing, but you're always basically still there. I can't begin to imagine how difficult it is to be an identical twin."

I swirled my cereal around in the bowl.

"I just don't like the same things as her anymore," I said. "I mean, snakes . . . ugh!"

My mom laughed. "I love snakes!"

I was surprised. "You do?"

"Yup. I had a few as a kid. They're fascinating and beautiful."

"Huh," I said, picturing it. "You did? So? About Isa?"

My mom sighed. "Isa is just trying on new identities, exploring new interests, and it's age appropriate. No one knows who or what they're going to be for life at your age. Let's just give her some space. The harder you chase her or push her, the more she'll dig in her heels. Just like that one!" She pointed at Cinnamon, who was battling Butterscotch, and we laughed. "The most important thing is that Isa is always your sister and you always love each other and stand by each other. Understand?"

I nodded. "I did try to protect her," I said softly.

"I know you did," Mom said. "Dad and I talked about that. And even though you lied and it wasn't right, I know you were covering for your sister. I understand how hard that must have been."

"I told her to tell you!" I cried. "What was I supposed to do? She trusted me!"

Mom looked at me. "I trust you. Trust is a big thing. Lying, even if you think you do it for the right reasons, never ends up being the right thing."

"I know that now," I said.

"And now you know that I like snakes too," Mom said, smiling. "Sometimes life is a little difficult. But you are loved by three people in this house, always, no matter what."

"I'm not so sure Isa loves me," I said. But it was weird. As soon as I said it, I knew it wasn't true. I loved Isa and Isa loved me. Sisters forever.

Mom and I cleaned up our breakfast and gathered our things. "I'll drive you to school," said my mom. "That way you don't have to run for the bus."

As I closed the kitchen door behind me, I took one last survey of the kittens.

Mama Honey was lying on her side, her tail flicking; Butterscotch was chasing Honey's flicking tail; and Marshmallow and Cinnamon were curled up together, fast asleep.

I looked for Isa all morning around school, but I never ran into her, which wasn't that unusual. What *was* unusual was that I didn't even see her at lunch. Now that she had new friends, she sat with them at a particular table every day, and that day she wasn't there. Did she hate me so much that she was even avoiding me at school?

I approached her table nervously on my way to return my tray. I cleared my throat and said, "Has anyone seen Isabel?"

The kids looked at one another, and one girl—I'm

pretty sure her name was Raven—said, "I think she's working on her science project in one of the labs."

"Oh. Okay. Thanks," I said.

I had a few minutes before my next class, so I waved good-bye to Tamiko back at our table, and to our other friend, MacKenzie. Then I headed off to look for Isabel on the science floor. In the second lab I spied her through the window in the door. Her head was bent over a tank filled with wood shavings. Mice. What was she doing?

I saw her teacher, Mr. Sacks (I had Mr. Bongort), come look in the tank from the other side. They stood there talking, and Isa was making notes in her notebook, glancing back and forth from her notes to the mice.

Huh. What was it with this girl and mice these days? Maybe she felt bad about feeding them to Naga? Maybe she wanted to know more about their nutritional value? I shuddered. Whatever it was, it looked like she was pretty involved with it, so I didn't bother her. I was just relieved that she wasn't purely avoiding me.

At dinner later she did finally appear. Granted, we were having chili, one of her favorites, so she could hardly have stayed away. The aroma had filled the downstairs of the house and then wafted its way up the stairs. My dad made the world's best chili.

I didn't say anything right away, but I resolved to learn more about her mysterious and all-encompassing science project.

Once we were all sitting at the table, with heaping bowls of hot chili in front of us and smaller bowls of shredded cheddar, sour cream, and chopped onion circulating, I pounced, just like Marshmallow.

"What's your science project, Isa?"

Isabel blinked hard in surprise, then narrowed her eyes and looked away. "Just something for our biology unit." She shrugged.

"Oh, interesting. What are your topics, girls?" asked my mom, digging into her chili.

I watched Isabel carefully. "I'm doing mine on carnivorous plants," I said.

"Wow! Exciting!" said my mom with a laugh, her hand in front of her full mouth.

My dad rubbed his palms in fake-evil glee. "Who will we feed to it first?"

"Dad! Those plants don't eat *people*. Just gnats and things like that."

"One can dare to dream," said my dad, returning to his chili.

I laughed. "Have someone in mind?"

He grinned. "Lots of people! Mwwaa-ha-ha-ha!" He imitated an evil laugh.

I glanced at Isabel and could see she was trying not to smile.

"What's your topic, Izzy-boo?" asked my dad.

She shrugged, then mumbled, "Genetics."

"Another good one! What are you researching?" asked my mom.

Isabel wiped her mouth with her napkin and cleared her throat. "Nature versus nurture."

"Very interesting. And what are you finding?"

"For some traits, nature is more important. For others, it's nurture."

"What does this mean again?" I asked.

"Sierra!" scolded my mom. "Weren't you paying attention in class?"

"We have different teachers. Isabel's is better."

"No excuses," said my dad, who was pretty stern about schoolwork.

Isabel barely looked at me, but at last she explained with a long drawn-out sigh. "'Nature' refers to how you're born—your genetics. 'Nurture' is how you're raised—your environment."

I actually thought that our biology class had learned about that.

"So, good news. I've found someone to take Naga, and he's a really good guy," my dad said.

"Phew!" I said.

"Why are *you* so relieved?" asked Isabel scornfully. "It's not like she was *your* responsibility." Before I could answer, I let out a little yelp of pain.

"Ouch!" One of the kittens had just attacked my sock-clad foot. I wiggled away and tucked my feet up on my chair, crisscross applesauce, as I used to say when I was little. "I'm just saying . . . ," I said.

"Well, *don't* say," said Isabel, stabbing at her chili with her spoon.

"He can come get her this weekend," continued my dad. "I said we could bring her to the clinic with us on Saturday and he could pick her up there. He's willing to pay for her, Iz."

Isabel looked up, surprised. "Really? How much? Not that I'd take the money," she added in a hurry.

"He offered seventy-five dollars for the snake and another fifty dollars for all the gear. You might want to take it," said my dad. "Think about it. You can donate it to a charity that helps reptiles."

Isabel looked thoughtful for a moment.

"You don't have to decide now," said my dad.

I decided to ask the question that Tamiko had been pestering me about all day. "What do you think about doing an adopt-a-thon at Molly's next Sunday, since the kittens will be eight weeks old? Tamiko would like time to publicize it if we're going to do it. Those kittens are so adorable; I bet tons of people will come."

Isabel rolled her eyes.

"What?" I said.

"Nothing," said Isabel. "May I be excused?"

"If you're finished, sure, honey. Just put your things in the dishwasher."

My parents agreed to the adopt-a-thon on one condition: that we do it from three to five so that they could wrap up things at work and then come supervise and approve the adoptive families. The families would all have to agree to give the proper care to the cats. My parents even volunteered to be the cats' vets, free of charge, for the first year. I was excited to clean up dinner and then race to text Allie and Tamiko.

Allie checked with her mom and reported that the adopt-a-thon was fine with her. Tamiko chimed in that she'd start working on the social media stuff and said that maybe we should all get together to make posters after school. I agreed and invited them to our house on Wednesday. Tamiko said she'd take a bunch of photos of the kittens that we could post, since "they're so photogenic."

Next Tamiko texted me on the side and asked if I thought we should ask anyone else to help make posters with us, like our new friend MacKenzie or even Amber, who'd adopted Gizmo the shih tzu. But sometimes Allie got kind of bummed when we invited other people to do stuff with us, because ever since Allie had left our school, she'd felt a little like we were replacing her with MacKenzie. So we had to be careful to keep it just the three of us sometimes.

We doled out assignments for what to bring on Wednesday, and the plan was set. At breakfast the next morning I asked if Isa wanted to help us with the posters.

"No," she said flatly.

Fine, I thought. *Be that way.*

Tamiko and I got to my house on Wednesday just as Allie's mom was dropping her off. The three of us piled into the kitchen, and I noticed that the door to the living room was already open and the kittens were roaming around in there. That meant Isabel was home.

"Hello?" I called. "Isabel?"

"In here," she replied from the living room.

Huh. Maybe she *did* want to help after all!

I offered drinks and snacks to my friends and even called in to see whether Isabel wanted anything, but she said no. Then I noticed that she was talking to someone. I poked my head into the living room, and there on the floor, among the kittens, were Isabel and her friend Raven from school—the girl who'd directed me to the lab earlier in the week. I said hi, and then I gasped.

They had Naga with them.

"Chill, Sierra," said Isabel, all cool. "It's fine."

"Isabel! That's not fine! That's like when two species collide! Like, this could turn into an episode from Animal Planet at any moment. You've got to put her away! I'm serious! Right. Now!"

Raven had Naga and was letting her crawl all over her shoulders and down her arm. The kittens weren't *right* next to her. Snakes move fast, and kittens can be clumsy, so it was not safe.

Allie and Tamiko followed me into the living room, and I braced myself for an awkward social interaction. But Tamiko said a friendly, "Hey, Isabel! Hey, Raven!" and Raven smiled and waved back. Isabel looked surprised that the two were friendly, and I quickly introduced Allie to Raven.

Isabel had a defiant look on her face, as if she were daring my friends to say something about the snake. She said to Raven, "Here, let me hold her for a minute," and she took Naga into her hands and allowed the snake to roam on her arms. She kept looking up at my friends, almost taunting them with the snake. But I was relieved to see that they didn't freak out.

"So this is the famous Naga, huh?" said Allie.

Tamiko squatted down next to Isabel. "Can I hold her, please?" Tamiko asked.

Isabel looked shocked. "Uh, sure! Just take her like this. . . ." She showed Tamiko what to do, and Tamiko took over.

"Hey! Do you mind if I get a photo?" Tamiko asked Isabel.

Isabel actually smiled. "Sure. Where's your phone? I'll take it."

I was frozen in the doorway, though. "Isabel, do you really think this is a good idea?" I asked. The kittens were wandering closer and closer; they were interested in all the people suddenly on the floor.

"Sierra, I said to relax. It's fine." Isabel stood and snapped some photos of Tamiko.

"Allie, do you want to hold her?" Tamiko asked.

Here comes the squealing for sure, I thought, but Allie surprised me too. "Sure. Just show me what to do. I'm scared. I don't want to drop her."

Isabel looked incredulous for a moment. Then she gave Allie a little lesson and transferred Naga from Tamiko to Allie.

My nerves were jangling as I watched the kittens and snake nearly interacting on my living room floor. It was as if Isabel and I were playing a game of chicken, trying to see who would back down first.

Isabel won.

I scooped up the kittens and brought them back into the kitchen and shut the door. Then I joined the circle on the floor around Naga, just like the one we'd had when my parents had first brought home the kittens.

Isabel was the happiest I'd seen her in weeks. Allie and Tamiko oohed and aahed over Naga and how beautiful she was, and Raven was pretty knowledge-able about snakes. She was also really nice. For about a half hour we all hung out and chatted and had a great time. It felt like the old days, back when Isa and I had been pals and had shared friends.

I didn't want to be a killjoy, but we had work to do. I finally suggested that we go in and use the kitchen table to do our posters, but Isabel nicely offered to put Naga away so we could stay in the living room and use the coffee table. Raven even offered to help, but Isa dragged her off to listen to some horrible music up in her room.

After they left, Allie and Tamiko looked at me with raised eyebrows.

"That was fun!" said Allie.

"That was the Isabel we know and love, back from the dead!" said Tamiko bluntly.

"I know," I said, shaking my head in wonder. "And all it took to get her back was a little snake-handling!"

We all cackled at that and got to work, but I did think about it later that night as I was going to sleep. Isabel had been civil to me at dinner. Maybe she just wanted someone to be excited about her new pet and her new friends and her new interests.

Maybe that someone was me.

CHAPTER NINE

ISABEL HAS A HEART!

Saturday morning Isabel and I were up super early to go to work with our parents. I dawdled at the kitchen table, drinking my hot chocolate slowly and letting Marshmallow play with the string of my hoodie. I was about to start getting sentimental about the kitties leaving us, when Isa walked in.

She was grumpy in the mornings, so I usually didn't try to speak to her, but today there seemed to be visible waves of grumpiness rising off her. I watched her thunk her bowl down onto the counter, shake cereal into it, splash milk over the cereal, and then slump at the table to eat. She pulled her hoodie up over her head and out, like the brim of a cap, so that I couldn't see her face.

Okay, whatever, I thought.

Cinnamon was trying to play with her foot, but Isa kept impatiently shooing the cat away. Finally I caved and spoke.

"Why don't you want her playing with you?" I asked.

Isabel glanced at me and shrugged.

"Is she annoying you?"

Isabel sighed and kept chewing.

"What's the deal?" I asked. I watched Isabel scoot her foot away again and lift her leg onto her seat. Cinnamon looked around, perplexed, like, *Where did my jungle gym just go?*

"Here, Cinnie!" I said.

"It's 'Monster'!" growled Isabel.

I lifted my chin. "I can call her whatever I like. And anyway, who made you the boss of her?"

"I picked her nickname when I named her."

"Okay, *mis amores!*" said my dad, hustling into the kitchen. "We need to head over now."

I stood, dumped my cocoa into the sink, and, in a rare moment of neatness, rinsed the mug out and put it into the dishwasher. I put on my sneakers, grabbed my phone, and went to sit in the car. I just wanted to be away from Isabel. As I sat there, I scrolled through all the posts that Tamiko had worked on. She was getting tons of likes for the photos of the kittens, fewer likes for the pics of the posters announcing the details of the adopt-a-thon. I suddenly had a pang. *What if no one comes tomorrow? Or worse, what if people come to play with the kitties but no one wants to take them home? Especially Honey, the grown-up cat.*

The tailgate of the car opened, and I could hear my dad and Isa maneuvering something. Of course! I'd forgotten! We had to bring Naga and all of her things to the clinic that day for the reptile guy to pick up. No wonder Isabel was in such a bad mood.

Once Naga was safely stowed in the back and everyone was in the car, we set out. My dad lectured us the whole way about helpfulness and willingness and cleanliness and all the "-ness" we needed for our punishment/job that day.

At a certain point my mom said, "Andres. I think they've got it."

My parents' busiest day of the week was Saturday because they had a double whammy: appointments for people who couldn't come in on weekdays, and then drop-ins of sick animals who arrived without appointments. The clinic had a front desk manager, Flor, who kept everything under control. She was able to manage aggressive people and animals, as well as scared and weeping ones, because she was tough—with everyone but us, that is. She'd been with our parents forever, so she had a soft spot for me and Isa. She was almost like an auntie to us.

"*¡Niñas!*" she cried, throwing open her arms as we arrived. I dove into them and let myself be squeezed and rocked back and forth. She took her name "Flor"—"flower" in Spanish—quite literally and always dressed in floral patterns, wore floral accessories, and decorated her entire desk area with flowers, both live and artificial. Her earrings and bracelets jingled as she released me and dove for Isa. Isa did not tolerate hugs and kisses, but she leaned in headfirst and allowed Flor to give her kind of a one-armed hug around her neck. This was Isa's version of an all-out hug-a-thon—the most she'd ever tolerate from anyone.

"*¡Ay, mami!*" teased Flor, wagging her finger with its inch-long purple nail at Isabel. "Still no hugs?"

Isabel smiled shyly and shook her head. Flor patted

her on the shoulder and sent us to the back to find Miguel, the vet tech who'd supervise us for the day.

Miguel was kind, but he was overworked and not great at sharing his job. He actually did not know how to ask for help; it just didn't occur to him. So Isa and I spent the next hour chasing him around with mops and buckets and rags, trying to see what needed doing. We had one puke cleanup and one cat pee and then had to package up two poop samples from sick puppies. I gagged on that one.

Around ten we went out to do a sweep of the waiting area. It could get a little hairy in there, literally, and it was packed. As we opened the door and dragged our cleaning gear in, I spied two identical twin girls sitting on the love seat, clinging to each other and crying softly. Between them was a big cat in a carrier who looked really unwell. I glanced at Isa to see her reaction, but she was looking away, as if scanning the room to see what needed cleaning.

I immediately felt a bond with the twins and felt so bad for them and their sick cat that I crossed the room to say hi.

"Hey," I said quietly, bending down. "Is your kitty sick?"

One of the girls nodded sadly. "She ate something bad."

"She's throwing up," said the other.

"Do you think she'll die?" the first one asked me.

"Oh! What? I don't work here. I mean . . . I'm a volunteer, just for the day, so I wouldn't know."

Suddenly Isa was beside me, and she squatted down too. "What did she eat?" asked Isa.

"A whole chicken salad sandwich," one of the girls said. "I left it on the coffee table in the living room when I went to the bathroom and I forgot about it."

"Oh dear," said Isabel. "That's not good."

"Mom always tells us not to leave food where the cat can get it," the other sister said. "And you always forget."

"I didn't mean it!" the first sister cried.

"I'm sure the doctors will make her better. Don't worry," I said.

A man came out of the bathroom and crossed the room to rejoin the girls. He smiled at me and Isa. "Twins?" he asked, pointing at us.

That hadn't happened in a while. When we'd been small, it had happened all day long. But since Isa had changed her look, most people didn't notice.

I grinned at the girls and nodded. "Yup. Just like you two."

"Identical?" asked the dad.

Isabel nodded. "Technically," she said.

The dad smiled. "I bet you two got into a lot of trouble when you were little, just like these two."

Isabel and I looked at each other, and she finally broke into a smile. "Yup," we said at the same time.

Isabel squatted back down. "You have to be nice to your kitty. Kitties like people to take good care of them and look after them. Just like you do with your sister. You take care of each other, don't you?" The girls didn't say anything for a moment, but then they both shyly grinned at each other and nodded.

"Well, we hope your kitty feels better soon," I said. As we walked away, I whispered, "OMG, that is totally something that would have happened to us. I'm always leaving snacks around the house."

Isabel actually smiled. "It definitely would have happened to us. If we'd ever had a pet!"

"Right?" I crowed, and we laughed.

As we were cleaning the waiting room, mopping the floor around people's feet, I saw a man come in without a pet. He approached Flor, and she interrogated him and then told him to wait. She scooted away from her desk, which is something Flor never does, and disappeared into the back.

"Isa?" I nudged Isabel. "I think that's Naga's new dad."

Isabel whipped her head over to look. "Really?" Her face showed a mix of emotions: anguish, concern, and hope.

We stood leaning on our mops and waited for Flor to return. When she did, she beckoned me and Isa over to the desk.

After Flor introduced us, the man said, "Hi, girls. I'm Herb Miller. Coming to adopt . . . is it Naga?" He smiled, and his eyes crinkled kindly, as if they got lots of smiling practice.

Isabel gulped nervously and nodded, while I stuck out my hand, as my parents had always taught us.

"I'm Sierra Perez, and this is my sister, Isabel. She's the snake lady."

"I'm happy to meet you both. Tell me about Naga," he said to Isabel. The two of them started chatting—Isabel tentative and shy at first, but then opening up and really talking with the man.

"And she really just loves to be held," Isa was saying when my dad came out.

He ushered us all back to his spotless office, where Naga's tank sat on his desk, with her heat lamp and humidifier all plugged in. She was curled up in her cave, and Mr. Miller squatted down to see her.

"Oh, wow, she's a beauty!" he said softly. "I can see why you picked her."

Isabel beamed. "Actually, I rescued her from a friend who couldn't keep her anymore."

"Kind of like he's doing for you," I said.

"Right," agreed Isabel, giving me a glance. I knew she was relieved that someone was taking Naga, but she'd never told Mr. Miller that she didn't want the snake anymore.

I wondered if Mr. Miller knew the real reason why we weren't keeping Naga.

My dad smartly moved things along. I knew he had a lot of patients waiting. And Mr. Miller had come from far away and had a bit of a drive home. Plus, I think Dad knew that Isabel was going to be sad. Even though Naga was going to a nice home with someone who would love her and who could care for her better than Isa could, it still didn't make it any easier for Isa to let Naga go. Saying good-bye was going to be hard.

Before we knew it, we were helping Mr. Miller load Naga into his truck. With the tank in the front seat, he asked Isabel if she'd like a moment alone to say good-bye to Naga, which I thought was super-nice. We all waited on the terrace of the clinic while Isabel stood on the running board of the pickup and whispered into the lid of the tank. When she stepped down, she quickly wiped a tear from her eye. I felt so bad for her just then. My dad had that look on his face that he gets when one of us is hurt, like he's hurting too.

Isabel gently closed the truck door and walked back to us, her head hanging.

"Hey, you can come visit anytime," said Mr. Miller. "And maybe when you're older and the time is right for you, you'll come get a new snake from me!"

Isabel nodded, unable to meet his eye. Dad wrapped his arm around her, and she buried her face into him.

Mr. Miller pulled out his wallet and peeled off a bunch of bills. He folded them and tried to hand them to Isabel.

"Oh, no. Thanks. I've thought about it, but I just couldn't. She was free," said Isabel, looking up now with her tearstained face.

"Well, you've had some upkeep and food and whatnot. Why don't you take half, and if you feel uncomfortable, you can donate it to the World Wildlife Fund for reptile protection." He handed her a bunch of the money and kindly patted Isabel's shoulder. Then he smiled at my dad and nodded. "Off I go."

My dad walked him to the truck, and we called our thank-yous after him.

When I turned back from waving, I saw my mom holding Isabel in a full-body old-fashioned hug. That was a new one.

I left them alone and went back inside to mop up more poop.

"As you girls know, when Papi and I have had a tough day at the clinic, we like to do something special to cheer ourselves up," said my mom early that evening. "We have to balance some of the sadness with fun at home. You girls worked so hard today and then came home and did your homework. And, Sierra, you looked after the kitties again. And, Isa, *mi amor*, I know how hard it was for you to give up Naga. What would you two like to do for dinner that would be fun? We could go out."

"Ooh! I know! Let's go to the mall and get bubble tea!" That was my favorite food treat in the area.

My mom nodded her head from side to side, considering it. "We could do that. Isa?"

Isabel shrugged. "I don't know," she said.

My mom and dad exchanged a worried glance.

"Sweetheart, we know you're upset about Naga . . . ," Mom said.

Isabel was more upset than I'd seen her in a long time.

"I have a plan," said my dad. "Let's go. Everybody, in the car."

"Where are we going?" my mom asked.

My dad leaned over and with a sly smile whispered into her ear. Her eyebrows shot up, and she said, "Good call."

As we drove away from the house, my dad said, "First stop: JumpOn."

"No way!" I cried. "Thanks, Papi!" JumpOn was an awesome indoor trampoline park that Isa and I had

121

loved ever since we were little. It had tons of trampolines and then a room that was entirely bouncy, so you could throw yourself against the wall or floor and bounce back. Plus, it had a whole soccer-trampoline room, where you bounced and shot, which was where we'd had our birthday party in fourth grade.

The best thing about going was that my parents didn't just sit and watch. They jumped too.

"Is there a second stop?" I asked, getting excited.

"Yes. After JumpOn, we're going to Sid's." He looked in the rearview mirror at Isa, trying to catch her eye. It was her favorite place to eat, so she should have been grinning from ear to ear.

I snuck a glance at Isabel and could see that she now had a pleased look on her face. It wasn't quite a smile, but it was good enough for me.

To say that we jumped would be an understatement. We jumped and bounced higher and for longer than we ever had before. Even Dad, who usually called it quits early, was jumping so high that I thought he was going to hit the ceiling. We did tricks and showed off for one another, and invented challenges and dares. We played two-on-two soccer, with Isa and me facing off against my parents, and Isa and I won.

When we got home, we were all exhausted but happy. Isabel seemed much better.

My parents announced that they were going to take showers and get into their pj's, and I did the same. Then I bounded down the stairs to have one last nighttime snuggle with the kittens. It was going to be so hard to give them up the next day, especially my mini-me, Marshmallow.

But when I reached the living room, they were nowhere to be found. Nor were they in the kitchen.

"Mami?" I called into my parents' room. "Do you have the kitties?"

"No, *mi amor*. Why?"

"Um . . ."

Where could they be? I didn't want to alarm anyone, but could they have been stolen?

Mom came out of her room with a puzzled look on her face. "Weren't they here when we got home? Did someone leave the outside door open?" She went and checked, but everything was locked up tightly.

We looked all around downstairs and didn't see them anywhere.

"And they weren't in your room?" my mom asked. "You're sure?"

"Yes, Mami."

Then she cocked her head and turned to the stairs.

"Mami, I said they're not up there!" But she kept walking up the stairs, and shortly I heard her knocking on Isa's door. I followed her up. "Mami, she won't know where they are. . . ."

But as Isabel opened the door, I could see all the kittens in her room. Tears were streaming down Isabel's face, and she had Cinnamon in her hands.

"Isa!" said my mom. "What on earth?"

"Oh, Mami. I don't want the kitties to go too!" wailed Isabel.

"Sierra, will you please excuse us for a minute?" asked my mom.

"Can I just grab Marshy?" I asked.

"Fine," said my mom. She held the door while I scrambled in to grab the kitten, and then she closed the door after I left.

I took Marshmallow into my room and played with her for the next half hour. I could hear the rise and fall of my mother's voice through Isa's door, and the occasional burst of Isabel talking, but I couldn't make out what they were saying.

Finally my mom came out and closed the door behind her. She looked tired and sad.

She sighed heavily and came to lean in my door-way, with her arms folded.

"Mami, I just realized. We never checked if these were boy or girl kittens!"

"Oh, right," she said, less than enthusiastically. "We should probably know for tomorrow." She crossed the room, lifted Marshmallow, and looked under-neath him or her.

"This one's a girl!" she said.

"I knew it! What about the others?"

My mom looked at Isabel's door and sighed. "Can I check in the morning?"

"Sure," I said. "I'm going to miss these little guys," I said.

"I know, *mi amor*. Me too. Sleep well."

CHAPTER TEN

SISTERS 4-EVER

It was another beautiful Sunday, and Tamiko was feeling enthusiastic about the adopt-a-thon! She texted
me bright and early to say that she'd had more than
two hundred likes for the adopt-a-thon, across var-
ious social media. I felt optimistic that we'd find
homes for all the kitties. Then Tamiko asked: Gearing
up for the big event?

I had to laugh when I read it. It's not for seven
hours! I replied.

Allie texted me too. We've had four calls at the
shop about the adopt-a-thon!

Great, I replied. But to be honest I was feeling
bittersweet about the whole thing. That night when
I got home, there'd be no more kitties. No animals at

all in the house. It would feel empty and sad.

I sat in the living room, letting the kittens crawl all over me, just like Isabel had done with Naga the other day. They were bigger now, and their ears had fully opened up. Their heads were still bigger than their bodies, which was cute, and their tails were the same size: skinny, skinny.

Butterscotch was playing quietly with a ball of my dad's needlepoint yarn, and Cinnamon dive-bombed her. Then Marshmallow came along to help out, and the three of them played tug-of-war with the yarn. I didn't see Honey nearby. She was probably resting somewhere.

My mom came in and sat with me quietly while she drank her coffee. We just giggled as the kittens did funny stuff. Then my mom picked up Butterscotch and looked underneath.

"Boy!" she said.

"Really? I can't believe it. I would have thought he was a girl."

"Why?" asked my mom.

I shrugged. "I don't know. I guess because he was kind of quiet and cuddly and not as wild as the other two?"

She bopped me on the head with her newspaper. "Silly. There are many quiet and cuddly boys. Grab Cinnamon."

I scooped up Cinnamon just as Isa was coming down the stairs, sleepily rubbing her eyes. I handed the cat to my mom, and she peeked underneath.

"A girl!"

"What? Really?" said Isabel in surprise. "I thought she was a boy!"

"Why?" asked my mom again.

Isa shrugged, just as I had. "I guess because she was so physical and adventurous and brave."

My mom smacked her palm to her forehead like my dad always did. "I've raised a couple of sexists! How did it happen? There's no saying that boys or girls have to be a certain way! Open your minds, girls! Your personality is not determined by your gender!"

We were quiet. We knew she was right.

"And it shouldn't matter at all if someone is male or female. Anyone can do or be anything they like! There's nothing predetermining you or holding you back!" Mom said.

Isabel spoke up. "Genetics *do* play a part."

"Yes, of course. And so does environment. Nature

and nurture. But please don't live by old-fashioned rules. Listen, if I did, I wouldn't be a vet. And Dad wouldn't needlepoint! And our lives would be that much worse for it. Right?"

Isabel and I nodded guiltily.

"Be open-minded, girls. Promise me."

"Okay, okay. They're just kittens!" I said.

She swatted me again. "You know that's not what we're talking about. Now go get dressed for church."

As Isa and I trudged up to our rooms, Isabel shook her head. "I can't believe Cinnamon's a girl!"

"Are you going to come help with the adopt-a-thon?" I hadn't wanted to ask, because I knew Isabel would say no and it would hurt my feelings.

And sure enough, she declined. "I have to work on my science project," she said, not meeting my eye. "I'm going over to Raven's."

"Okay . . ." I turned to walk away. "Well, you could always come if you finish. Bring Raven. Everyone likes her."

"Thanks," said Isabel. "I won't. But thanks anyway."

After church and a quick brunch, Isabel hugged and kissed all the kittens and Honey, their mama, and wiped a tear from her eye as she said good-bye. Then she took off to go to Raven's, and I got ready to go to work. My parents would swing by the clinic for a bit—their renovation was almost done—and then come home, pack up the kittens, and meet me at Molly's at two forty-five.

Tamiko and Allie were already at work when I arrived at twelve forty. I was proud of myself for being early again, even though Allie hadn't requested it. I thought I could figure out this on-time stuff sooner or later.

Tamiko had the stacks of fact sheets about the cats all ready to go. There was only one problem. We hadn't filled out whether the kittens were boys or girls.

Allie frowned at me. "People will want to know if they're adopting a male or a female."

I sighed. "Get me a pen."

I sat and filled in the info about the kittens on their sheets.

Meanwhile, Tamiko was prepping the ingredients for her cat sundaes. She cut piles and piles of Nilla wafers, then sorted the M&M's into blues and reds and put them in separate containers. Then she refilled the squeeze bottle of chocolate sauce, wiped the drips from the side, and set it neatly next to her workstation.

Allie and I replaced two tubs of ice cream that were low and wiped all the tabletops. This was our slow time, but we knew it would soon pick up. We were all nervous and excited for the kittens to arrive and had high hopes for the adopt-a-thon.

By three thirty we were in full swing! We had a long line out the door of people waiting to order. My biceps ached from scooping ice cream; Allie's fingers flew over the keypad of the cash register, ringing sale after sale; and Tamiko—who usually spent half her time chatting with the customers—barely said a word, she was so busy creating her specialty sundaes (cat-themed, unicorn-themed, and more).

Outside, my parents sat at a table with the cats and the flyers, surrounded by posters. I watched out of the corner of my eye as people stopped by to chat, and many of them played with the kitties. My parents had brought a clipboard with adoption forms from the clinic, but I didn't see anyone filling anything out. Part of me was thrilled—yay! We'd have the kitties at home again that night!—and part of me was sad and hurt—didn't anyone want our kitties? I thought they'd be gone in a flash.

At four o'clock it was time for me to take a break. The line had shrunk a bit, and Mrs. Shear came out from the back to relieve us.

"Go on outside, girls, and get some fresh air. Also, get an update on the adoptions!"

There were still a lot of people milling around the cat table, eating ice cream. Tamiko and Allie and I scoped it out, eavesdropping and watching.

There was a young couple considering Honey, who had nestled into the woman's arms and fallen fast asleep in the sunshine. They looked pretty set on her. I was super-happy that a family wanted a grown cat; I'd worried that no one would. And then there was a family playing with Marshmallow, which made my heart pinch in a way that really surprised me. They looked nice enough, but was their daughter a little too rough with the kitten? Was their son disinterested? I felt very critical as I watched them. As we were standing there, a mom with a young son who was holding Butterscotch came over to the table.

"We'd like to take this one, please," said the lady. She seemed very nice, and the little boy was enchanted by the cat. He held him so carefully, and the expression on his face was so joyful that it actually brought tears to my eyes.

I nudged Allie. "So cute," I whispered.

"That's my kitty!" joked Allie.

"I know. And that one's mine," I said, gesturing at Marshmallow.

"And that one's mine," said a voice behind me.

"Isa! I thought you weren't coming!" I said, spinning around. Isabel stood there with Raven, who was smiling and saying hi to Tamiko.

"We needed a break from our science projects, and I thought ice cream was a good idea."

I squeezed her shoulder. "Come inside. What can I get you?"

We entered the shop, and I showed Isa and Raven around and explained all our specials. Tamiko and Allie washed up and hopped behind the counter.

Isa ordered another snake sundae—with a smirk—and Raven ordered a peppermint shake.

"Coming right up!" said Tamiko.

I wiped the tables and counters and refilled the

straw and napkin dispensers while Isa and Raven chatted with my friends. I was so happy that they had come. It felt good.

Once Isa and Raven had their ice cream, Tamiko and Allie shooed us all outside, saying with a wink that I could supervise outside and pick up any trash, but they knew that I just needed some more time with the cats and with my sister.

A really cute boy had arrived with his mom and was standing chatting with my parents. He was a little taller than I was and had huge sea-green eyes with the thickest, longest eyelashes I'd ever seen on a boy. I listened in to hear what they were saying.

"Yes, they've all been adopted. I'm so sorry," my mom was saying. "But the shelter van will be here next Sunday, and I know for a fact that they have a whole passel of kittens, because we just referred someone to them last week."

Wait. What? All the cats have been adopted?

I felt panicky—I needed a chance to say good-bye! I looked around and saw that the couple with Honey had already left—and taken her with them! Oh no!

"Isa! Did you hear that?" I said frantically.

Isa was also looking aghast. She nodded. "OMG. This is really the end." She set her spoon back into her ice cream dish, too stunned to keep eating.

"Let's say good-bye to them all again, okay?" I said.

Isabel nodded.

First we went to the little boy holding Butterscotch and asked if we could say good-bye. He agreed, and Isa and I each took a turn holding Scotchy and whispering into his ear.

Then we held Cinnamon one last time before her new family came back to pick her up. My dad had Marshy on his lap, so we scooped her up and snuggled her. I was choked up as I gave her one last kiss on her fluffy white head and handed her back to my dad.

"Who adopted her?" I asked.

"A nice family with two girls," said my dad. "They're getting here later."

"And Cinnamon?" asked Isabel.

"The same family!" said my mom.

"So the sisters will stay together?" I asked.

My mom smiled. "Yup."

I looked at Isa. "Well, that's a silver lining anyway."

"Yes, it would be so sad if the sisters were separated," Isabel said.

"Sisters for life," I whispered. Isabel looked at me for a moment and then gave me a small smile.

She knocked her knuckles against mine. "Team P," she said quietly.

As my parents chatted with the remaining people about cat care and their clinic, Allie's friend Colin from her new school arrived, as did Amber and MacKenzie.

"Are we too late?" asked MacKenzie.

"You missed meeting the mama cat," I said. "The kittens are still here, but they've all been adopted."

While Colin busied himself arranging photos of me on his phone, Allie, Tamiko, my parents, Mrs. Shear, and the kittens for the school paper, Isabel and Raven hung out with Amber and MacKenzie. Amber was updating Isa on Gizmo, and her stories were making Isabel laugh. I was happy to see Isabel cheering up, though I still felt hollow inside at the loss of Marshmallow.

Soon it was time to wrap it all up. The cute boy—Amir—promised he'd be back the following Sunday, which made my stomach feel woozy in a happy way. My parents sorted out the paperwork for everyone.

And Tamiko, Allie, and I popped back inside for a final cleanup. I saw Isabel and Raven helping to move the table and chairs back inside and packing up the posters and flyers while my parents said good-bye to Mrs. Shear.

Then I said my good-byes to Allie and Tamiko and headed outside to say good-bye to Raven, who was getting into her mom's car.

Finally it was just the four of us outside: me, Isa, my mom, and my dad. My dad had the kitten box with Marshmallow and Cinnamon in it, and he was getting ready to put the towel over it.

"When is the family with the two girls coming back to pick them up?" I asked, looking at the time on my phone. "Do we have to wait?"

"I hope not! I have to get home and finish up my science project for tomorrow," said Isabel.

"They're already here," said my dad.

I looked around but couldn't see anyone. Confused, I said, "Where?"

"Right here!" laughed my mom.

I looked at my dad. He had a huge grin on his face.

"Wait . . . ," I said.

"What?" asked Isabel. It was taking her a tiny bit longer to process, but *I* knew what my parents meant.

"Mami, are they . . . are we keeping them?"

My mom nodded, beaming. "Yup. One for each of you!"

"Whaaaat!" Isa and I screamed at the same time. We threw our arms around each other and started jumping up and down. Tamiko and Allie came running out of the shop, wondering what was going on and why we were celebrating.

"What's happening?" asked Tamiko.

"We're keeping Marshmallow and Cinnamon!" I cried, tears streaming down my face.

"OMG!" Allie threw her arms around me and hugged me tightly. "You finally got a pet!"

"Awesome!" said Tamiko.

"Oh, Mami! I can't believe it!" I hugged my mom and then my dad, who still had the kitten box in his arms.

"Thank you both so much!" said Isa.

"But why?" I asked. "Why now?"

My parents looked at each other. "Let's discuss it on the way home," Mom said. "These kitties need a break."

We said good-bye again to my friends and hopped into the car, which was parked up the street.

Isa and I buckled our seat belts. Then we took our kitties and snuggled them next to our cheeks at the exact same time, in the exact same way. We were both so happy.

My parents, who had turned to watch us from the front, laughed. "Once a twin, always a twin," said my mom.

"So why did you suddenly decide we could have pets?" I asked.

"Yeah," said Isabel. "Why?"

My dad cleared his throat. "First of all, we felt that if we had created a home where people had to sneak around to get what they wanted"—he looked meaningfully at Isabel, who ducked her head—"then maybe we were being too strict. Then we had the kittens, and you both took great care of them."

"Even going so far as to take them to work with you," chided my mom.

"Which was a bad idea," added my dad, "but at least it showed us how seriously you took the responsibility. And how much you wanted them to have good homes."

"As did Isa's excellent care of Naga," Mom continued.

"Then, when Isabel no longer wanted Naga . . ." My dad trailed off.

I whipped my head to the side to look at Isabel. "So you really didn't want her in the end? It wasn't just that she was too much work?"

Isabel shook her head sadly. "It just wasn't me, having a snake. I mean, she was a cool snake and everything, but she wasn't really the kind of pet I wanted. Plus, the kittens were so much more fun to play with, especially when other people were over. They're just a happier kind of pet."

"I thought Naga was cool," I offered.

Isa shrugged. "Totally. But then there was the frozen mouse aspect. . . ."

"The mice-icles?"

"Mice pops?" Isa said, grinning.

My mom groaned. "Anyway, we saw a lot of strong feelings from both of you about sisterhood, and what it means to be a sister and stick together."

"And the cats seemed like a good way to reinforce the importance of sisters," summed up my dad. "We just couldn't separate them."

I sat back, Marshmallow now sound asleep on my lap. "Wow. I just cannot believe it."

Isabel nodded. "This will take some getting used to. But I'm glad we have some new members of Team P!"

"Kitties for life!" I joked, and we did the knuckle bump. I looked over at Isa and she was grinning at me. I hadn't seen her look so relaxed and happy in a really long time.

After dinner and a shower, I sat in my room with Marshy until my parents called us down for our Sunday night show. We were watching a series on TV, and the second season had just been released, so we were pretty psyched. My parents liked for us to have a show going at all times; they said that it bonded us as a family.

"Come, girls!"

I scurried down in my pj's with Marshmallow and sat in my usual chair. My parents were on the sofa.

"Isa!" called my mom.

"Coming!" she yelled.

Isabel jogged down the stairs with Cinnamon in her arms. "Just finished my project!" she crowed.

"Wonderful, *mi amor*!" said my dad.

"What was your conclusion?" asked my mom.

"Well, identical twins have identical genes, so most of the time they're exactly the same in looks and mannerisms and things like that. Some traits are more identical than others—like identical twins will always have the same eye color and hair color—but other traits are more variable, like math skills and personality. Those might depend more on environment and preferences."

"Wait," I said, surprised. "Your study was on *twins*?"

Isabel shrugged. "Yeah?"

"I thought it was on genetics."

"It was. It's just that genetics studies usually use twins for research, because of the shared genes."

"So what was your research question?" I asked.

Isabel looked embarrassed for a second. Then she said, "Are identical twins exactly the same for life?"

I looked at her closely. "Obviously not!" I said. I could feel my parents watching us.

Isabel nodded. "I know. I just wanted scientific proof that some of the way twins act is by choice and some isn't."

"What part isn't by choice?"

"That identical twin sisters are twins for life." She smiled.

"And what part *is* by choice?"

"That they're friends for life!" said Isabel, knocking her shoulder into mine.

"No matter what?" I asked, also smiling.

"No matter what," said Isabel.

I thought about it for a bit. We would always be identical twins, but that didn't mean identical thoughts and feelings. Isabel would always be her own person, and so would I. And I was fine with that.

Team P forever!

DON'T MISS BOOK 4:
ICE CREAM SANDWICHED

I put the finishing touches on my book review as the school bus pulled into Vista Green School.

"Perfect Pairing," I typed into my tablet. "Eat a scoop of banana ice cream sprinkled with toasted coconut to taste the flavors of Barbados. Although, I'm pretty sure that the Puritans did not approve of ice cream!"

Puritans, ice cream, and Barbados. Okay, that sounded a little weird. But I'd selected *The Witch of Blackbird Pond* as my first book to review for the school newspaper, the *Green Gazette*. I'd chosen it because I'd thought it would be good to start with a classic, and this book had won an award (a Newbery Medal, which was a big deal for books). *The Witch of*

Blackbird Pond was about a girl from Barbados who, in the 1600s, moved to New England and had to adapt to a Puritan lifestyle. I'd checked to make sure the school library had a copy of it, in case my review inspired anyone to read it.

My new friend Colin was the paper's assistant editor, and it had been his idea for me to add an ice cream pairing to each review. I knew that book reviews didn't usually include food pairings, let alone ice cream suggestions, but my mom just happened to run the newest ice cream parlor in Bayville. Colin knew that I liked to suggest ice cream flavors to customers by asking them about what books they liked. So he'd thought it would be fun to do that as a newspaper column.

I hadn't waited until the last minute on the bus to write the review; I'd tweaked the piece at least seven times already, wanting to make sure it would be perfect before I submitted it to Colin. But today was my deadline, which meant now or never, so I took a deep breath and uploaded it to the shared drive just as the bus came to a stop.

I was still fairly new to Vista Green, and I didn't have any real bus friends yet except for Amanda. Amanda, her mom, and her sister lived in the same apartment building as my dad. But I got to sit on the bus with her only when I was staying with my dad, and today I was coming from my mom's house.

If that all sounded confusing, that's because it was! My parents had gotten divorced right before I'd started seventh grade, and even though they were being very cool about it all and didn't scream at each other or anything like that, I still hadn't quite adjusted. They had sold our old house in the town we used to live in, and so most days I lived with Mom in a beach bungalow near the ice cream shop, while the other days I lived with Dad in a high-rise apartment with a pool on the roof. It might sound cool to have two houses and two rooms, but I didn't quite feel at home in either place yet.

My new address at the beach house in Bayville also meant that I was going to a different school from my friends, who all went to Martin Luther King Middle School, which was one town away. In my heart, I still felt like I was a student at MLK.

Luckily, I'd managed to make a few friends at Vista Green: Colin, Amanda, and Eloise, who sort of came as a package, I guess. I wouldn't exactly call them nerdy or geeky, but they were definitely not part of the cool club at Vista Green. And by that, I mean that they didn't dress the same and have the same opinions as everyone else, something I'd seen a lot of at my new school.

At least, that was what I'd thought. But that morning, I would learn that the Vista Green Fall Frolic was one event that had just about everybody at the school falling in line.

After I got off the bus, I headed to my locker. For the first time I noticed the Fall Frolic posters plastered on every sage-colored wall I walked past. And everyone was talking about the dance too.

"I have been waiting for this since last year!"

"Did you get your dress yet?"

"I still haven't found the right shoes!"

A few feet away from my locker, I saw Amanda getting her books out of hers.

"Hey, Amanda," I greeted her.

She looked up and smiled, her brown eyes friendly through her black-framed eyeglasses.

"Oh, hey, Allie," she said. "What's up?"

"It seems like everybody is talking about the dance," I said. "Is it a really big deal here?"

I had the bad luck of asking the question just as

two girls were passing by: Blair and Palmer. Colin liked to call them the "Witches" but I was starting to think that doing that was insulting to female practitioners of the magical arts. Because there was nothing magical about Blair and Palmer and their other friend, Maria. They were usually just mean— although Blair was by far the worst offender. That was why I had nicknamed the group the "Mean Team."

The girls both stopped in their tracks.

"Is it a big deal?" Palmer repeated, with a flip of her long, straight, brown hair. "It's only the biggest event of the year!" She turned to Blair and asked, "How could she not know that?"

Blair responded with a flip of her own long, straight, sandy-brown hair. "Maybe she's too busy dishing out ice cream at Mommy's store," she said, and then she and Palmer walked away laughing. It actually did kind of sound like cackling, so maybe Colin's assessment was correct.

I was steaming. MLK wasn't perfect, but there I'd had the safe little bubble of friendship with my best friends, Tamiko and Sierra. MLK had a lot of different groups of kids and not one big Cool Club. You could kind of do your own thing, and I'd never had to worry about being a mean-girl victim.

"Well, that was lovely," Amanda said dryly, and then the bell rang.

I headed off to my first class, science with Ms. Conyers. She wasn't my favorite teacher at Vista Green—that would be Ms. Healy, my English teacher. Ms. Conyers was supersmart and kind of reminded me of Ruth Bader Ginsburg, the Supreme Court justice, with her small frame, pulled-back hair, and big eyeglasses. But Ms. Conyers could be a little boring sometimes, even though we were studying Earth's geological history, which should have been really interesting.

It turns out, though, even Ms. Conyers was excited about the Fall Frolic.

"Is anyone in this class on the music committee of the dance?" she asked, and a boy named Logan raised his hand. "Please make sure there aren't too many slow songs this year. I could not get my groove on last fall."

She mimicked a funky dance move, and everyone laughed. Maybe she wasn't as boring as she seemed. As the morning went on, I realized that the Mean

Team was right—the dance was a big deal. In my next class, Italian with Signore Bianchi, we all learned how to say, "Are you going to the dance?" *(Stai andando al ballo?)* And in art class a small group of kids from the dance committee worked on decorations while the rest of us had our regular lesson.

When it came time for lunch in the cafeteria, I was anxious to get the scoop from my Vista Green friends. Amanda, Colin, Eloise, and I sat at a table with Preston and Haruo, two boys Colin had been friends with since kindergarten. The three of them were, like, best friends, so they usually spent the whole lunch period talking with one another and ignoring us.

"So, the Mean Team set me straight this morning," I began as I unpacked my lunch. Then I filled Colin and Eloise in on what had happened. "I guess this dance really is a big deal."

"Well, first of all, ignore Blair and Palmer, as always," Colin said. "But yeah, I guess it is kind of a big deal here."

Eloise nodded in agreement, her blond curly hair bouncing on her shoulders. "It's a really big deal," she said. "Everyone dresses up, and they hire a professional photographer and DJ. It's pretty cool."

Amanda rolled her eyes. "I guess. If you like that kind of thing."

Eloise nudged her. "Oh, come on, Amanda. You like it just as much as everybody else."

Amanda frowned and ate a bite of her sandwich.

"You said everyone dresses up," I said. "Just exactly how dressed up do you mean?"

I was thinking of the sixth-grade dance at MLK, which was pretty casual. A lot of kids just wore jeans and nice shirts. I'd worn a dress and regular flats, but not a fancy dress.

"Well, all the girls shop at that boutique in Upper Springfield," Eloise said, and Amanda rolled her eyes again.

"What boutique?" I asked.

Eloise started tapping on her phone. "It's called Glimmer," she said. "Everyone gets a short dress, not a long one. And everyone gets thin straps."

She showed me a photo on her phone of a model wearing a slinky silver above-the-knee dress with very thin straps. It didn't look like a dress I would ever wear—unless I was going to be walking the Hollywood red carpet. And it definitely didn't look like a dress Mom and Dad were going to let me wear.

"Does everyone dress like that?" I asked.

Eloise shrugged. "Most girls. You look out of place if you don't."

"Even you guys?" I asked.

Eloise nodded, and Amanda bit her lower lip.

"It's just . . . I like dancing," Amanda replied. "And this way I don't have to stress about what to wear. I just go to Glimmer and pick something out. It's easy."

"And then we fit in," Eloise added. "Which is not a bad thing, because we don't normally fit in around here."

"I don't know," I said. "That kind of dress is just not . . . my style."

I looked over at Colin, to see if he had an opinion, but he had inserted himself into the conversation between Preston and Haruo. I guessed that the topic of girls' fashion wasn't his favorite.

"You should get over to Glimmer soon," Eloise suggested. "All of the good dresses go early."

"Thanks," I said, and I thoughtfully dug into my salad. Once again I wondered what my life would have been like if my parents hadn't divorced and I were still going to MLK. I knew that the MLK seventh graders got more dressed up for dances than the sixth graders, but I was pretty sure that short, grown-up dresses weren't mandatory.

I sighed. Even if the dresses hadn't been an issue, I knew I was going to miss being at the dance with Sierra and Tamiko. I was glad that I'd met Colin, Amanda, and Eloise. But Amanda and Eloise were best friends already, so I usually felt like a third wheel when just the three of us were together. And Colin was great, but he was a guy—and hanging with Colin was not the same as hanging with my two best girl-friends, whom I could share anything with.

I was so happy that Sierra and Tamiko had agreed to work at my mom's ice cream shop every Sunday. I was guaranteed to spend time with them at least one day a week. But one day a week still didn't feel like enough.

I missed having my Sprinkle Squad around me every day!

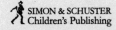